I0538249

PAPERBACK VERISON

ISBN-13: 978-0615915876
ISBN-10: 0615915876

To order additional copies of this book, contact:

Cover design by: AMB branding design
www.ambbrandingdesign.com
shauntakenerly.wix.com/shaunta-presents
shauntakenerly@yahoo.com
https://www.facebook.com/michael.hixson.90?fref=ts&ref=br_tf

Please leave a review

"Don't Knock it Till You Try It"

Michael Hixson

It's amazing how we pass by a lot of treasures that are right under our noses. We do that in the cities that we live in. We pass by the same shops often. When we are driving, we are in tunnel vision, such as is in life. Your friends say, "Hey, come to my grand opening of my restaurant." You ask for directions and they say, "Right next to this place or that place." You're confused because you never took the time to find out the name of that place or the name of the street. The embarrassing thing is that you've been passing by this place for years. There are historical places, sites, and facts that we fail to know because we don't take the time to research. We're always thinking that amazing is a concept or a thing that is abstract or afar; something not right under our nose. The same thing goes for dating.

Hollywood has flooded us with this image of what our mates should look like. We see these pro athletes, Jet Magazine beauties of the month, rappers, singers, and models thinking that's what our mate should look like. However, this shouldn't be the case. After all, these people are airbrushed. There are people out there that keep having unsuccessful relationships and are dating the same personality type over and over again. They subscribe to the idea that you have to kiss a thousand frogs before you find your prince or princess. I found in my research that it's not always that the person doesn't want who they are pursuing. They are worried about what their family, friends, and others will think if they will choose this type of person. However, life and true love situations don't ask for permission.

Fed Up

Keisha and her girls are discussing their current relationships. They are all fed up with their men. The relationships are ones that are endured because of longevity but not enjoyed. Happiness is gone, but rather than leave, the girls felt like they should just let their love lives die a slow death.

This is a casual affair. Each girl is wearing their college t-shirts along with matching pajama pants. The girls are all gathered at Keisha's house. The house is on the outskirts of the city. The ladies are sitting in the house. The house is a very upscale dwelling. There is a Chinese garden with a water fountain and a pond outside. The walkway outside has a chamber that contains tons of African art. There are the African masks as well as ebony statues. On the outside, the house itself looks like a Mexican Villa with the smooth white stone finish and Spanish tiles on the roof. There are walk way stones that lead to the main entrance. Her bedroom has a European theme. There is a great canopy bed, and the bed spread is of the finest materials trimmed with gold lace. The sheets are silk with pillows that are not like any other with gold stitching. There is a big glad sliding window that leads to a balcony that offers a great view of the city. At night, the buildings are lit with orange lights. The common area that Keisha and the girls are sitting in is a huge chamber that contains a large screen TV. The walls have multiple paintings that contain paintings of the ocean and relaxing beach scenes. The ladies are eating bon-bon's watching chic flicks. The movies are really watching them. Not only are there bon-bon's, there are Reese's cups, M & M's, smoothies, ice cream buckets, and milk shakes.

This is a therapeutic, bad love type of detoxifying eating session. There are candles burning, and the ladies are beyond relaxed. They are fresh out of a relaxing bath, and their aroma is like a love spell of scented lotion along with their soft skin, making them as fresh as newborn babies fresh out of the tub. They clearly are fed up with their current situations. A wise man once called this the rebellious stage, which is the point where someone in a rut decides enough is enough.

Keisha is a very light brown-skinned, thick woman with long jet black hair. She is considered the leader of the group. Donique is the sassy yet fun-loving, humorous one of the group. She has a caramel complexion while Tasha is the soft sweet gentle one. Tasha grew up in a house that was plagued with verbal, physical, and emotional abuse. Her mother had poor self-esteem, so in an attempt to repair herself, she often married sinister/sadistic men that took advantage of her. Growing up is this type of environment caused Tasha to develop a compassion for victims of abuse as well as those that were deemed social pariahs. She vowed to treat people with tenderness. The tone, volume, and cadence of her voice is often soft and therapeutically empathic. She has a short light-skinned petite frame. Sensitivity and compassion are her mantras.

Lena is a Janet Jackson thick sista with cinnamon colored hair and skin that is the color of a perfectly cooked pancake. She's like the model Jessica White. Her personality is a dichotomous one. She's a hybrid between Hilary Banks and Thelma from Good Times. She can be smart and sophisticated and hang with the upper echelon on topics of politics, business, and other things. However, if need be she can fight and argue with the best of them. She is "Ms. Understanding."

"Chris is not a bad person. He buys me anything I want, but he's always running the streets. I just want something more," Keisha says.

"I know what you mean girl. When me and Tyrone are talking our conversations are limited. We talk about music and clothes and nothing else," Tasha stated in an empathetic tone.

"Uh-huh girl, I'm feeling both of y'all. Malik and I go out to eat and I feel like it is out of habit," Donique replied.

Michael and his friends are discussing their non-relationships. They're all geniuses. All scored perfect on their SAT's. However, all are clueless when it comes to females.

"I'm tired of having my hopes up every year saying, "This year I'm gonna get this girl, that girl and when the time comes not doing or saying anything," Michael says with a voice of disgust.

7

"Yeah or going out to the movies or to a restaurant, watching some couple holding hands or gazing at each other giggling," Anthony says with a look and feeling of emptiness in his voice.

"No offense guys, I think it's getting old that all of us sitting together building, programming software and calling that fun," Johnathan says in agreement.

"And let me add watching Star Wars or reading comics. Even Superman had Lois and Spiderman had Mary Jane," David says in and the, "And the church says amen" voice.

The girls, their men, and I use that term loosely during one-on-one discussions. The girls are trying to define their relationships as well as explain what they are unhappy with.

Chris is sitting on the couch with a, "Nobody better not say nothing to me" expression on his face He is daydreaming about how he is going to take over the whole city. He is strategizing and itemizing his moves. He's trying to think of how he is going to classify his henchmen. He knows how good his men are but he wants to organize an elite force of the best of the best sharpshooters that will personally guard and protect him. He does not care about how his drug dealing is affecting his woman.

Chris was locked up for a few years, and during his incarceration, Keisha stayed faithful to him but being faithful clearly is not what he is doing to Keisha.

He is allowed to have multiple women. However, if Keisha even remotely looks like she is admiring another man, he runs up with his gun drawn in a crazy rage. One day the police smashed down Keisha's door with a battering ram along with the SWAT Team looking for Chris. They had no regards for her property. They smashed expensive vases, tore rare paintings, etc all in an attempt to find dope. There have been numerous occasions where Russian, Chinese, and Latin drug lords shot at him and his women while they were out trying to have a good time. His antics were so taxing on Keisha that she had a nervous breakdown which eventually lead to the miscarriage of their child. Chris is one of the city's main dope boys. He has dread locks and a muscular frame. Chris grew up in a dysfunctional home. His mother was strung out on crack, and he had an absentee father that ran the streets selling drugs and chasing women.

"Chris I feel like I want more," Keisha cried as tears stream down her face in a deep pleading voice.

"What do you mean more?" Chris says with a "What are you talking about?" stupid look on his face.

"It seems like you don't love me," Keisha says.

"Love you? Don't I buy you anything you want?" Chris says in a rhetorical manner.

"Yeah but real love is more than buying gifts. It's about spending time with your woman," Keisha says in

9

voice that's trembling and one step away from crying.

Chris responds with an arrogant, "I'm God's gift to women" expression on his face, "You trippin! There's a lot of girls out there who would love to be in your place. I'm leaving. There's too much money to be made and girls who will appreciate a guy like me who makes it!" Chris stomps off slamming the door so hard that a picture of them falls off the wall and the glass frame breaks.

Tyrone is a full time self-employed mechanic. He's been working on cars since he was ten. Busted knuckles and cramped hands are familiar friends to him. By the time that he gets home, he is exacerbated. He's just gotten home from a long day's work. He still has his work clothes on. His uniform has oil splashes on it as well as stained steel toed boots. He has issues expressing his feelings, so he often takes it out on his woman.

"Hey Tyrone how was your day?" Tasha asked out of genuine concern.

"It was aight," Tyrone replied quickly with a closed in statement as to avoid further conversation.

"What did you do?" She asked trying to spark deeper conversation.

"I went to work. Talked to the guys," he says this while looking in another direction and walking. He then gets up and heads towards the T.V.

"Don't you want to know about my day?" Tasha questions like a little girl wanting her daddy's attention.

Tyrone is laughing sarcastically, "Your day? Get serious. You do the same thing every day," he replies in a smart mouthed manner.

"Talk to me baby. Tell me about your hopes and what you want out of life," she says in a whining voice.

"Alright," he says with an "I give up" sound in his voice.

She feels happy because he appears to have given in. "I want you to move out of my way so I can watch this fight," he stands up and points with a look in his eyes as if he wants to slap her.

Malik is wearing the best clothing that money can buy. He's so clean it hard for him to function. His hair has an extra crispy razor line. Malik would be great at ninjitsu because the objection is the distraction or delusion. Malik has a credit score of 480. He is 3 payments behind on his current car payment. The car company smelled him from a mile away. He was given a car with an interest rate of 29%. His payment is $500 a month, and his rent is $600. The problem is that he only makes $800 a month. He prances around in expensive suits talking on his cell phone trying to appear important. However, half of the time he's on the phone talking to creditors. Malik is constantly investing his money into pyramid schemes and other unsuccessful ventures. He's spending money recklessly because he borrows from his woman to fund his impractical dreams. The irony in this is that he looks like he wants for nothing. However, his woman is often nickeled and dimed by him and is emotional needed and destitute for love.

"So what are we going to do tonight?" Donique asked in an anxiously excited childlike anticipatory voice.

"You know what's up," he says with a "don't get it twisted" look on his face, "We'll go to the Chicken shack and maybe watch a dollar movie. Why change it?"

"Let's do something spontaneous. Exciting," Donique asked.

"I know how bout you buy this time. For both things," Malik responded with sarcastic excitement.

"Chris told me there are a lot of girls out there who want to take my place. All I want is quality," said Keisha.

"Tyrone would rather watch the fight on TV that the one we had in our living room," chimed in Tasha.

"Malik played me cheap. He says he wanted me to pay for a cheap date. It's bad enough he wants to take me on a cheap date and make me pay for it at that."

Lena walks in very fast and anxious. You can feel the tension from her. Her very presence changes the climate of the room. She has her hands on her hips. She is shaking her neck and her finger as she points and talks, "I don't know about y'all, but I'm tired of all these no good brothas. If y'all are as tired as I am, let's go ahead and try this new thing." She passes the flyer to Keisha. Keisha reads the flyer aloud, "This paper says they're looking for people who are ready to try new things in love. An all expenses paid cruise and hotel week."

"All expenses paid!" Donique and Tasha simultaneously yelled.

Michael runs in frantically. His motions and breaths are preceding his words. He's bubbling over with excitement like a pot of boiling neckbones, "Hey fellas you says that you're tired of being lonely. You guys ready?" He quickly asks. His boys have looks on their faces that show the fear of the unknown. Anthony reads the flyer aloud, "All expenses paid cruise and hotel week." David and Jonathan chime in simultaneously as they look at each other quickly with enlarged, amazed eyes, "Were in!"

Keisha and the girls are going shopping. Michael and his boys want to change their image. So, they go shopping as well.

"Now y'all know we gotta get some new outfits," Keisha emphatically says. "New shoes," Donique

13

quickly states.

"New bathing suits," Tasha says as she jumps in competing for air time.

"Aren't y'all forgetting something?" Lena says as she wiggles her fingers and toes, and points to her hair.
"We're gonna go from geek to sheik, Michael says looking forward as if into the future.

"Well I got some friends in Saudi Arabia," David says oh so seriously but in a spaced out manner.

"No we're gonna go shopping!" Michael says as he grabs his forehead.

"No doubt fresh!" Anthony passionately says.

"That's wassup," Johnathan says unconsciously.

"I like where this is going. Fresh. That's wassup," Michael says with a Captain look who is about to venture into new uncharted waters in his eye.

It's a hot and sunny day. The girls pull up in an all black reflective paint Mercedes. They walk up giggling and talking like a bunch of seventh grade girls getting ready for the big dance. As they enter the door, the blast of air conditioning feels like they walked in a fast food. They could smell the aroma of Mr. Chang's Chinese food.

The girls go to purchase heels. If heaven were a

14

shoe store, this is what it would be like. Keisha holds up a pair Cinderella shoes, "I'm definitely gonna get these. These are some Cinderella fairy tale type stuff."

"Lord knows we kissed a lot of frogs," says Donique then laughs.

"It's a shame none of them turned into Princes," says Tasha as she laughs.

"We're not waiting on Prince Charming. We gone jack that dragon up our daanng self and get to the happily ever after," says Lena.

Each girl tries on 3-4 dresses in a 3 way mirror while friends say, "Yea or Nay". Finally, after each girl has received the approval of her companions, they moved on to their next phase of fashion screening.

The guys walk into a hip hop gear shop. "What up Bruh? What you need?" asks the clerk.

"We were hoping you could tell us," says Michael with a lost look on his face.

"We want to look fresh?" says Anthony waiting for confirmation.

"Were about to take a trip, and we want to look good for the ladies," Johnathan says jumping in to remove the ambiguity.

"Yeah," says David.

"Come with me," the clerk says.

David picks up a pair of Jordan's. "I don't know guys," he says.

Michael interrupts, "We're gonna put our best foot forward."

Anthony picks up a pair of Air Force 1's. "I think I really know the meaning of Fresh," he states with big eyes.

Jonathan points to a nice button up shirt. "Now that's wassup!!" he says with his mouth open.

Girls are under the blow dryers at a hair salon. Keisha is taking on the leadership role for the trip. "We need to set some ground rules," she says.

"What kind of rules?" Tasha asks as if the idea is abstract.

Keisha answers her back, "About when we get to the trip."

Lena jumps in, "Let's hear it."

"Run 'em by me," Donique asks in speculation.

"Let's not go out. They're going for the same type of men we left. Let's be open-minded. Let's try some of the shy brothas," Keisha says in a suggesting mother voice.

16

The boys simultaneously walk out of dressing room. "Now that's what I'm talking about!" says the clerk. As the boys exit the store, they pass the girls. The boys go to the shop in an urban environment. The door opens and the boys have nervous looks on their faces. The barbers are laughing and come to an abrupt stop.

"How can I help you gentlemen?" asked Ray.

"We're about to go on a trip," says Michael.

"What kind of trip may I ask? Business or pleasure?" Ray replied.

"We're gonna see some girls," blurted David.

"We're trying to look our best," Jonathan says.

"We're nerds. Any advice with the ladies?" says Anthony in all honesty without concern.

"Confidence," says Phil a fellow barber.

"That's right!" Ray interjected.

"We're not exactly smooth with it," says Michael with concern in his voice.

"It's not about smoothness. I got two words for you. Do you!" advised Chuck, the barber in the far chair.

"The problem is dudes ain't got no courage. They scared somebody not gonna accept them, and they start trying to be fake and impressing them," says Ray with a sincere disgust in his voice. The guys sit there as if they are in a lecture. They literally take notes as the barbers talk. Then they leave armed and dangerous with the do's and don'ts of approaching women.

The Trip

The Night Before all the girls sleep over Keisha's and all the boys sleep over Michael's. "I wonder if we'll find Mr. Right tomorrow?" asked Keisha with an exhausted expression in her voice.

"Yeah hopefully we will. The main thing is to get away from here and have fun," says Tasha with a sound of solace and comfort in her voice.

Michael's Convicting Speech

"When we get there I'm gonna give it all I've got!" says Michael in his conqueror voice emphatically.

"What do you mean?" asked David with an absolute clueless look and tone of voice.

I'm gonna approach and talk to the girls I don't ordinarily talk to," he says with his chest stuck out and head held high.

"Yeah. Don't knock it till you've tried it!" says David in amazement of his own statement.

"Yeah! That'll be our motto," says Michael.

Keisha and her girls as well as Michael and his boys are in the airport and one step closer to their voyage that is going to change their life forever. "We'll this is it!" says Keisha looking at all her girls to see the expressions on their faces and verbal responses.

"I know I'm so excited!" says Lena flailing her arms.

They all group hug and scream with excitement and jump up and down simultaneously.

"Well gentlemen the time is here. Bring it in. All guys circle up and put fists in. Don't knock it till you try it!" says Michael in his quarterback and captain of the football team voice.

"I like that!" says Johnathan as he nods in agreement.

"Yeah me too! Who came up with that?" asks Anthony.

"My main man Dave," says Michael as he looked toward David squinting with intensity like you know what we've got to do in his eyes.

"That's our theme!" David says in a Justice League declaration tone.

The girls walk in their room with their mouths wide open. There are white curtains, sheets, and carpet. The ceiling is white with gold trimming. It looks more like a gothic cathedral than a hotel room. Edible fruit that look like flowers are on tables in baskets. Silver platters are laid out with extravagant meals waiting under the tops. The bathroom has a tub shower and Jacuzzi. Lena walks in and flops on bed. "Aaah! This is nice!" she says in her calgon relief voice.

"Check out the view," says Tasha as she overlooks beach.

"I want to see the view alright," says Donique as she looks with suggestion in her eyes.

Keisha looks at Donique, "Girl you so crazy!" she says as she laughs.

The boys prepare to enter their room. They think it will be a nice plain hotel room. They are in for a rude awakening. Upon entering the room, they are realizing they have walked into the man cave of all man caves. The large flat screen TV makes it look like they walked into a cinema. There are tables with wings and portable stereo to keep it warm. Black forks and plates line the table. The sheets and bed spreads are black. Black and white checkered marble line the bathroom floors with a black marble tub and shower. Anthony speaks in utter awe like a child in a toy store, "Wow wireless internet!" he says.

"Cable TV!" says Johnathan with equal excitement.

"They're showing a Star Wars marathon tonight! David says with a childlike excitement."

"Remember why we came here gentlemen," Michael states in a redirecting tone then continues, "We can do that anytime back home."

Anthony picks up a paper off the TV stand. "You mean like this?" he says as he hands the paper to Michael.

21

Michael reads the letter aloud, "Thank you for being a part of this experience. Please report to the banquet room to receive your gift and packages and further itinerary."

Keisha notices a paper on the circular table in the middle of the room. "Here's your view," says Keisha as she reads the paper aloud, "Report to the banquet room to pick up your package and itinerary."

The girls accept the mission and they advance towards the banquet hall. The gold double doors catches everybody's eye. They smile with excitement and walk faster towards the door. A heavy set gentleman opens the door for Keisha staring at her body. The rest of ladies laugh at his gawking.

The girls are sitting on the other side of room of the banquet hall in the corner. The boys are up front as if in class. A gentleman passes out a package to everyone. The host begins to speak, "I'd like to thank everyone for coming. In your packages, you'll find your spending money and ticket for the cruise and itinerary. Don't panic, the itinerary is optional. Have fun. We'll give you a few days to relax and enjoy."

Lena snatches the package from Keisha's grasp. Keisha smacks her lips in disbelief. Lena, waits for Keisha or any of the other girls to say a word but they don't.

Lena slowly unties the bow on the package and

quickly start pulling out gift certificates, and other papers before handing each girl their tickets. All of them become so excited that they are hugging each other and practically crying.

After a few closing remarks from the speaker, the ladies hop up from their seat and walk towards the exit. Keisha notice Michael and his entourage walking behind them also leaving. He looks at her bashfully. Keisha cannot control her emotions and send him a wink but Michael thinks she aiming at another man behind him.

The girls continue to talk amongst themselves about the fellas until they enter the elevator.

On The Beach

The boys are walking on the beach. The beach has white sand with water so clear that you can see to the bottom. There are beautiful ladies in bathing suits everywhere. All the men look like bodybuilders or male fitness models. There are little walk up huts that are serving refreshments. People are playing catch football, volley ball, tossing beach balls, and Frisbees. Little children are building castles in the sand. The air is laced with the scent of tropical food frying. This is a beach playground for adults and children alike.

"Isn't this great?!" Anthony says unable to curb his enthusiasm.

"Yeah!" says David with equal or greater passion.

Jonathan with absolute incontinence shouts, "I can't wait to see the ladies!" "Yeah fellas this is it," Michael says as a general looking over next potential conquest site.

The ladies are walking with model like confidence. "Alright ladies let's have some fun," says Keisha like a coach laying out x's and o's.

"I think see some fun I want," says Donique while staring at guys.

Lena is cracking up laughing. "You need to stop," she says.

24

"Let's mix it up a little and try new things," Tasha says in her suggestive voice.

The fellas are walking on the beach and a ball rolls in front of David's foot. Fellas look up and see muscular street ballers with do-rags, tattoos, fancy cars, and athletic gear. 360, basketball icon yells to the fellas, "Hey Bruhh! My boys over hear talking smack! I told 'em I could beat 'em with any team. They don't think so."

The other ball players chuckle and waive their friend 360 off. "Y'all playin' or what?" he asks with an aggressive but welcoming tone.

David looks at Michael. Michael picks up the ball and chest passes it in. "You're on!" Michael says.

360 gives the introduction and welcome, "Meet the fellas. This is Earthquake, Fire, Trainman, Sky, and that's Handles."

Michael gives his lighthearted introduction and welcome of his crew to show respect but fun, "I'm Michael (AKA) 'Spider.' That's David (AKA) 'The Giant Killer'. That's Anthony (AKA) 'Pretty Tony'. That's Jonathan (AKA) 'Big John Stud.'"

360 chuckles and nods, "I like those names." The street-ballers don't realize the geeks have skills just as they do.

"Ball in!" 360 says with confidence.

"No shot stay back," says Rain Man in disregard of Anthony's skills. Anthony swishes the shot all net.

360 looks Rain Man dead in the eyes, "No shot huh?" he says running back on defense.

Rain Man giggles in mild embarrassment, "Beginner's luck."

Earthquake dribbles and crosses David over, "Shook him!" says Earthquake in a very bragging manner.

"That's alright!" 360 says confident that they will get them back on the next play. Michael throws alley oop and John dunks it in. Crowd shouts, "Ooooh!

Donique pulls out her binoculars. Keisha looks at Donique laughing. "Girl I know you didn't," she says to Donique. It's ironic that there is a game being played because 4 guys walk up that clearly need to work on theirs.

Guy 1 offers his pick up line. "The weather isn't as hot as you!" he says.

Guy 2 tries to redeem the group, "The lake don't sparkle like those eyes!" (As if the other lines weren't bad enough)

Guy 3 jumps in, "Sand ain't as soft as your skin I

bet!"

Finally Guy 4 tries to make his last what he thinks is a valiant effort, "And the view ain't as pretty!"

Tasha starts to advance towards the guys. Keisha steps in front of her and says, "See, its lines like those that got us in trouble in the first place."

"You right," Tasha replies.

"Let's see what's going on," Lena says as she looks toward the basketball court.

All of the girls walk up to the court. Donique says in her "why don't we explore it voice", "It's some brothas out there."

"Uh huh," says Lena.

"Let's holla," says Tasha.

It's apparent that the other girls have already forgotten Keisha's earlier words of wisdom.

Keisha almost gives in herself. "Not bad at all. However, let's give it a little time." she replies.

Back at the Court

David crosses Earthquake and drives to the hole for a score. "Whooo!" shouts David in jubilation. The next 3 buckets are hit by Fire, Rain man, and Handles. "Fiiire!" Fire sings the tune by The Ohio Players.

"Let it rain!" says Rain Man.

360 gets a fast break and does 360 slam dunk. "See how I got my name," 360 says to David. David has an amazed look on his face. Next Sky does one handed Tomahawk slam. "The Sky's the limit," says Sky with a pun intended towards his name. Handles stops on a dime repetitively dribbles then scores. "Bet I can do it again," Handles says. Handles steps in and steals ball. He tries a move. Michael steals the ball.

"Hey Mike, You been settin' everybody else up. It's your time to shine," says 360. Michael looks at 360 in agreement. "Bet," he says. He runs up the court, catches, and shoots to win game.

360 jumps up and down to rub the victory in. "Ooh! Ooh! Ooh!" he says walking up to his opponents. The guys give handshake/hugs saying, "Good game." "Hey fellas. I'm having a BBQ later on today. Y'all wanna come through?" asks 360. "Well…" says Anthony. Hesitantly Michael jumps in and interrupts him almost immediately then abruptly says, "We'd love to." Michael and his boys walks off.

As soon as Michael and his crew walk off, Keisha and girls walk up. "What's jumpin fellas?" says Lena. "Nothin. Y'all comin to the BBQ?" he asks.

"I didn't know we were invited," says Keisha with an impressed and honored look on her face.

"Yeah we comin'," says Donique almost immediately after Keisha's reply.

"Uh huh," says Tasha nodding in agreement.

"Well then, see y'all tonight," says 360.

The girls are at their room deciding what to wear. All you see is dresses flying in the air and shoes also. The women are walking in and out of the restroom waiting on their girls to give them their approval. "Let's be jaw dropping!" says Tasha.

"But classy," says Lena.

"Let's turn some heads!" says Donique.

After taking a deep breath and a pause Keisha says, "But most of all let's be ourselves."

All the other girls reply one by one in synch "Yeah!"

Michael and the fellas are for the most part ready for the BBQ. There is a smoke screen in Michael and the boy's room. No, it's not a fire. It's cologne. It's surprising that gas masks and bio hazard suits aren't being issued out to handle the strong smell. Michael is spraying cologne. "Gotta make sure I smell good," he says.

Jonathan is sitting on the bed with hands folded. "Huhh! Huhh!" sighs Jonathan.

"What's wrong Jonathan?" asks Michael.

"I am nervous about this BBQ thing. I mean I don't do social gatherings like this," says Jonathan .

"Me too! I don't know what to talk about other than Star Wars, comics, and things like that."

"He does have a point," says Anthony.

"This is like Star Warz," Michael says.

"Huh?" says David with lost look on his face.

"Before Anakin became a Jedi or Luke, they had to train or practice. This is our practice for a bigger event," says Michael.

"I get it. Excellent synopsis," says David having an "Aha" moment.

The BBQ

360's BBQ is a grander event than they all could've imagined. Guests are in the living room talking. Others are outside sitting at picnic tables or standing by the pool. The doorbell rings. Michael, Anthony, Jonathan, and David are at the door. "What up fellas?" says the man at the door. "Were here for 360," says Michael. The fellas had polos jeans and tennis shoes. They were in their laid back, subtle but dangerously good looking gear.

They all walk through the house outside past other guests. The house was decorated heavily with basketball trophies, pictures of a 6 year old toothless 360. There were high school basketball picture of a scrawny 360. There were framed jerseys. In its own right, the house looked like a miniature basketball hall of fame.

360 and the other players from the previous game are circled up talking and reenacting game and laughing. As soon as Michael and his buddies walk outside, they are smacked in the face by the aroma of barbecued chicken, hamburgers, ribs, and hot dogs. The side items look so delicious that it appears that they can be eaten by themselves. There are baked beans with bacon layered on top. There is potato salad with deviled eggs sitting on top and dusted with paprika. The desert table looks like a bakery all by itself. The plethora of cakes makes it look like somebody's grandma delivered for the occasion. There is cheesecake, birthday cake with icing spackled on oh so right, there is chocolate cake

moister than morning dew, and icing that's richer than Oprah Winfrey. There are coffins of ice coolers, and the punch bowls look like public pools are lined up. "Hey 360, more guests," says the man at the door.

"Mike! Fellas! What up Bruh? Come on over here!" says 360 in his "I can't believe you're here" voice.

"We're over here talking 'bout the game. Meet the fellas. You already know them," He points at Rain man, Sky, Fire, Handles, and Earthquake, "This is Mike, Dave, Anthony and Jonathan." Each guy mixes with other fellas, gives their names, and shakes hands. You can see Mike and his boys' discomfort.

The doorbell rings. The Doorman answers door. The girls look great from head to toe. The girls have on their summer but not too dressy dresses. "We're here for 360," says Keisha.

"Right this way ladies," says the doorman as he looks the ladies up and down with a slight smile. As the ladies walk outside to find 360 and the others, "So Dave comes back and shakes Earthquake," says 360 re-enacting the event. The fellas almost falling out laughing and hi-fiving says, "More visitors 360!" yells the doorman. All the fellas turn with strong attention. "Hey ladies. We got drinks and food. Help yourself," says 360 in a warm friendly and respectful manner. The other fellas except Michael and his click run up and start talking to Keisha and her girls.

Michael and 360 have 1on 1 talk. "So Mike

where'd you learn how to ball like that?" asks 360.

"Well my cousins were what you call "Hood". So I would tag along where they would go. Wanting to get picked up caused me to sharpen my skills. Unfortunately, the streets were where they wanted to play, and I'm sure you know that the streets don't play fair," Says Michael.

"That's true. But real talk, you and your boys are book smart but y'all have a little hood in y'all. I like the fact y'all ain't fake. Y'all are yourselves. That's what's up," 360 says.

This statement is one of confirmation and validation for Michael because he knows that 360 knows about the other side of the coin. This is sort of a knighting for him or a right of passage.

"How bout you?" asks Michael.

"Basketball is my life. Been playin since I was 5. I still want to give the league a shot. In college, I got into some trouble and had to quit."

"You should try the league," says Michael.

"Well Mike let's socialize with the guests," 360 suggests.

Michael and 360 walk back into the center of the back yard.

Anthony walks into the house for a second and notices two girls sitting on the couch with a space in between them. One girl pats the couch signaling him to sit down. "You smell good!" says the first girl.

"What you got on?" the second girl asks.

"Burberry," replies Anthony.

"So where you from?" asks the first girl.

"I'm from the great city of Dayton, OH," says Anthony.

"Dayton, OH?!" the first girl asks in a ridiculous voice.

Anthony replies, "Yeah".

"So what brings you here?" the second girl asks in amazement.

"Well my friends and I are on a vacation. So enough about me. Where are you ladies from?" Anthony asks.

"Here?" both girls reply simultaneously and unenthusiastically.

David and Jonathan are standing back and observing.

Anthony replies, "You didn't sound so excited."

"Well... I just wanted to see the world," says the first girl.

"Me too," says the second girl.

"So what's holding you back?" asked Anthony.

"I don't know," states the first girl.

"I'm a little scared," states the second girl as she sighs.

"Just remember you're the one that has to think about it when you lay down at night," Anthony says in a closing statement style.

The girls looked at Anthony with an endearing look. They knew he was a good guy. They were even more amazed after they heard his conversation. They were so used to men just trying to hit on them. It was refreshing to hear a man that was sincere and genuinely interested in their welfare. Anthony was amazed after he realized what he had done. He had talked to two attractive females. It was one thing to talk to one. It took him great courage to build up the nerve just to talk to one woman. This was like winning the battle then going to war. This was the start of a geek revolution and renaissance.

Keisha and girls are discussing the party. "There's some nice guys here," says Donique.

"Yeah there are," Lena replied in agreement.

"They're a lot different from the dudes were used to talking to," says Tasha.

"Yeah but something is still missing," says Keisha in her deductive reasoning voice. Keisha adds more. "It's like that outfit that will be that bomb stuff if it has one more accessory. A bracelet, a belt, earrings, or something.

Everyone's leaving including Keisha's crew and Michael and his boys. "Aight den Mike hit us up on myface.com or space book," says 360 bidding his new found friend farewell.

"Alright. Thanks for everything," says Michael.

"Bye Ladies," 360 stated to Keisha and the rest of her friends.

Keisha, Donique, Lena, and Tasha (simultaneously): "Bye!"

Beauties and The Geeks: The Cruise ship

The cruise ship is as long as 3 football fields. It looks like a floating skyscraper. Everyone looks up at the ship as if it were an angel from heaven that landed on the water. You can tell that whoever funded this cruise sacrificed all their time, talent, and treasure into this venture. "Tickets! Tickets! Have your tickets ready!" shouted the ticket clerk. The boarders had looks on their faces that kids have when Willie Wonka takes them to the candy factory for the first time.

The girls are standing in line giggling. The guys are talking in an excited manner. "Our first cruise," says Michael as he sighed looking up into the great beyond.

"Isn't it great?" David says in hyperactive manner

"You know it!" replied Anthony emphatically.

"This is more exciting than the starship battle Luke Skywalker went on," says Jonathan.

The dramatic and situational irony of this is that the boys and girls are a few spots in line right by each other.

"Beautiful view," says Tasha.

"Boat ride," Lena says looking up in amazement.

"The Brothas," says Donique.

The inside of the ship was just as spectacular as the outside.

This boat's interior makes the love boat look like a life raft. They have a restaurant on every floor. There are weight rooms on deck. There are internet cafes and coffee shops. There are spas and massage parlors. Even the servers are great because they have insurmountable manners. The waiters and waitresses inundate you with replies of "Yes ma'am, yes sir" and "I would be glad to." The deck floors are cleaned to perfection and glistening. The scent of fresh food simply invades the air. There are no depressed faces on the boat. Everyone looks approachable. Even the captain and his crew have pleasant expressions on their faces.

All four ladies laugh simultaneously at the outspoken Donique's reply. A voice speaks over the intercom. The Announcer says, "Your attention please. Your attention please. Now that all passengers are aboard we will now depart. We will cruise the beautiful Caribbean. Hope you all enjoy and thank you for traveling Festival cruise lines." All passengers cheer. Guys, girls, and others are standing in the commons area. A woman announcer's voice over the intercom says, "Could all the passengers with the special promotion packs please report to the ballroom immediately." The people start moving in single file line into the ballroom.

They find a young woman in her mid-late 20's standing in front of them. They are excited. They move forward gleefully with excitement like children who have their permission slips signed and are going on a field trip. They feel like VIPs that have the velvet rope lifted voluntarily for them. Never in Michael and the boy's lives nor Keisha and the girl's lives have they had this feeling of being in an elite group.

Now they will be amazed even more. Normally Dr. Hampton only attended ventures like talk shows and seminars that are for the most prestigious events Dr. Hampton is a gorgeous woman. She has long black hair and a light complexion. She appeared to be a model posing as a therapist. She went into the profession because she was one of the girls that dated the wrong type of men, so she devoted her life to stopping people from making the same mistakes that she had made. Dr. Hampton is a story within in a story. There could be a book wrote about her by itself.

Doctor Hampton introduces herself. Hello my name is Dr. Hampton. I am a PhD and a graduate from Southwest Ohio University. The reason you all are here is because we're running an experiment. We have divided you into groups and carefully selected you because we know that you would not have met or even spoke to each other if you were not in a controlled environment like this one. Don't worry. No weird science or hocus pocus. I left my lab coat and test tube at home." "I've devote the majority of my work looking to improve the lives of others. Especially in the area of finance. The crowd laughs. Dr. Hampton continues, "There will be tons of social events. 'Don't knock it till you try it', so let's break and everybody have fun".

Michael and his friends approach 4 girls. At first look at these girls compared to these guys, the guys felt the girls were out of their league because these ladies were drop dead gorgeous. The girls were so gorgeous that outsiders looking in would think that if the girls were interested in Michael and his boys that they were simply messing with them to take advantage of them. The climate of the room changed when these girls walked in. They had on shoes, purses, and clothes that the average person could not spell let alone pronounce. They stood tall and had laser beam focus into and through the person that they put their attention on. By the way they stared, it was hard to tell whether they were giving an x-ray, MRI, or just looking at people. "I came here to meet a balla," stated the first girl.

"I heard that! I want diamonds," The second girl replied.

"A new car!" the third girl added.

"A house!" says the fourth girl.

"So what up wit y'all?" asked the first girl.

Michael began stuttering and looking left to right, "Uhhh. We're good." "Yeah," says David.

"Me too," Anthony quickly replied.

"Well...maybe," Jonathan says entertaining the thought for a split second.

David, Michael, and Anthony simultaneously shout, "Jonathan!"

"Ok," David reluctantly stated. The guy clearly knew after their statements that they had fallen amongst ravenous she-wolves.

Keisha, Tasha, Donique, and Lena are approached by four friends. These guys looked like discount players. The rings and earrings they had on looked like they were made out of crystal. These guys are walking with a limp so severe, as if they were knee surgery patients that just got off the operating table. They were not crippled. They were just trying too hard to be cool. They were nodding, looking the girls up and down, and circling them as if they were sharks in a feeding frenzy. "What up with it?" says guy 1.

"Hey baby," says guy 2.

"Bye baby," says Tasha.

"Sup Mami?" says guy 3.

"Nothing's up wit it," says Keisha.

"Mmm! Mmm! Mmm!" says guy 4.

"Nothin Daddy?" says Donique.

"No, No, No," says Lena.

Michael and his crew are checking into their

rooms, at the same time that Keisha and her friends are checking into their rooms. David, Anthony, and Jonathan had the dejection and fatigue in their eyes of soldiers that had to retreat from battle. Michael was the strong floor general. "Man that was rough!" says Anthony.

"Yeah this meeting women business is rough!" says David.

"Tell me about it!" says Jonathan in agreement.

"Listen to yourselves. So what we had a bad experience! Let's go for it! Remember we came here to be brave!" says Michael with disgust and conviction in his voice.

"I'll try," says Anthony unenthusiastically.

"Yeah," says David in a bland tone.

"Yeah me too," says Jonathan.

"Try?! Try?! Try?! David what did Yoda say to Luke Skywalker?" says Michael with a ridiculous look on his face.

"There is no try. There's only do," says David.

"I didn't hear you!" says Michael.

David repeats the statement with more conviction, "There's no try. There's only do."

"That's right!" says Michael pumping his fist in the air.

Keisha and her girls are getting situated into their rooms. "Man it's like we're back home again!" says Tasha.

"Man!" says Lena.

"I feel you girl," says Donique.

"Listen to yourselves! What's the motto?!" says Keisha with disgust in her voice and throwing her hands up in the air.

Donique, Lena, Tasha say the statement in a murmuring voice simultaneously, "Don't knock it till you try it." Keisha shouts like a drill sergeant, "I can't hear you!" Donique, Lena, and Tasha shout the statement with the belief "Don't knock it till you try it!" They screamed.

At the he restaurant social Michael and his crew meet Keisha and her crew for the first time. Keisha leads the charge. "Look around girls. We gon' do it different. We not gon' wait to be walked up on."

"Who we gon' talk to?" says Lena sincerely searching.

Tasha is looking around at guys. Some guys have big smiles and are nodding and winking. "Uhh! Uhh! Nope," she says.

Donique locks in on Michael and his crew like an apache fighter helicopter preparing to fire hydra missiles, "How 'bout those brothas?"

"Alright. They look nervous. We'll push 'em a little," says Keisha in her "why not?" voice.

Keisha and the girls approach the table. Michael and his crew are very anxious and uneasy. They look like woodland creatures such as rabbits that are being approached suddenly in their own natural habitat. The bad taste in their mouth from the last loss has them somewhat apprehensive. This whole night was an absolute dream come true. The ambiance was set up perfect. No one could lose. All around were walking contradictions. There were esquire magazine looking men talking to girls with glasses and laptops. There were women that looked like they belonged on the cover of cosmo talking to guys that looked like they belonged on the cover of geek weekly. There were men and women that looked like male and female rappers talking to guys and girls who only attended ivy-league colleges and never left the suburbs. Had it not been for this event, a lot of people would not have ever conversed.

One of the funniest couples was Nathan and Markita James. Remember them for later. Markita James was in and out the prison system. Her crime record was like a resume. Grand theft auto, burglary, larceny, and identity theft are her smaller crimes. The whole night she looked around thinking, "Who's gonna be my victim?" She means this in an affectionate way.

She scans the room like a cyborg robot looking for a target then she spots Nathan. "Jack pot!" she thinks. Markita has to come up with a set up. She has the perfect plan. She brushes against him picking his pocket. She then walks up to him with his wallet in her hand and says, "Sir, I think this belongs to you."

"Why thank you! There aren't many honest people out there like yourself anymore," Nathan replies.

"I know what you mean," she giggles on the inside.

If anyone knows dishonesty and things of that nature, it's her. However, this time she's going for a second chance; second chance metaphorically and literally.

"Hey fellas, how are y'all?" says Keisha.

Michael, David, Anthony and Jonathan reply sporadic but simultaneously, "Good, Alright, and Ok."

Keisha begins introducing her friends, "This is Lena, Donique, Tasha, and I'm Keisha."

As the girls are introduced, the guys rise to shake hands. The gentlemen didn't know it, but this gesture of respect, standing in the presence of a lady was earning them points already. The girls were thinking that it's impressive to see men that are honoring them as ladies. Michael began introducing fellas, "That's David, Jonathan, and Anthony. I'm Michael."

"So what's jumpin with y'all?" Donique says.

All the guys look at each other in a confused manner. They know a little bit of slang but the little bit they know isn't much. If they began to speak it, all they would sound like is someone reading from a discontinued version of a college ebonic textbook.

"She means what series of events have transpired with y'all, and how are you doin'?" says Keisha.

Michael and his crew respond simultaneously after having an "Aha" moment, "Oh ok. Nothing much."

"So where y'all from?" asks Lena.

Jonathan starts steppin' up with happy look in his eye, "We're from Dayton."

"Really which part?" Tasha asks.

"Crown-Point," replies Anthony.

"Oh really?" says Donique with her head kinda cocked back in a surprised manner looking with a surprised look in her eyes.

Donique and her friends never would have guessed Crown-point. They would have guessed Oakwood, Englewood, Kettering, or Centerville. David chimes in, "Yes really, and to answer your question, my heart is jumping since I see you."

Donique is kind of blushing because she can see the sincerity in his eyes and knows it's not a line. "Forgive us ladies. Where are our manners? Where are you from and what brings you here?" Michael says.

"Believe it or not we're from Dayton also," says Keisha.

"We wanted to get away and try something new," says Lena.

"Yeah the guys we dated had no sense of spontaneity," says Tasha in relief to know that she can talk to someone about it.

"Not to mention insensitive to our needs," says Donique like a child tattling addition information.

"We want to break out of the shyness and talk to more ladies," says Jonathan

"So, how's this trips batch of boys been for you?" says Anthony.

Keisha began grabbing her forehead, "They had lines that sounded rehearsed."

"Like bad cue card readers," says Michael chuckling.

"Exactly. I to be so close with my love interest that when I talk, they can... can...," says Lena.

47

Jonathan politely started interrupting, "Finish your sentences."

Lena smiles at Jonathan as he smiles back. The music begins to play. Each girl yanks the guy of their choice between the fur men onto the floor. Hip hop music plays.

On the same cruise, there was another event going on. Jade Frost, an extremely wealthy self made millionaire, was holding an event for her group "The Ice Queens". Jade Frost is a man eater. She absolutely refuses to submit or be controlled by a man. Jade grew up in a home with a single mother. Her mother worked 3 jobs to provide for her and her 2 younger siblings while she was young. She would often see her mother crying when she would see the utility bills, rent notice, and doctor's bills. Later on, Jade ended up dating a man that was 12 years older than her.

This man was smooth. He knew how to manipulate and con to get anything he wanted, even Jade. At first, he started out to be nice. He would buy her nice clothes, cars, and everything else. Then one day he decided that he wanted someone else. He tried to talk Jade into dating him still while being with another woman. Jade finally refused after tolerating his unfaithfulness for a while. She decided to model for a brief period of time. However, this ended up being a scam. Her talent coordinator, a lady that appeared to be her friend, ended up secretly marketing her talent and selling to another guy. She was taking Jade's money, splitting it with this other mysterious gentleman, and

Jade ended up with nothing. These prior experiences caused Jade to become hardened and not to ever want to submit to anyone especially a man.

The Ice Queens was an extremely expensive dating agency. Jade was in charge of sending her Queens out on dates with rich men. Jade paid for their clothes, hair, and nails. These rich men paid for everything else. Jade was extremely protective of her queens. She would always track where they were through a GPS system. Wherever the girls were, there was an all black car with trained ex-special forces military body guards waiting for the signal. The Ice Queens themselves were also trained killers. She picked only the smartest and prettiest girls. Jade is gorgeous. She looks like Stacy Dash but better. Jade is skilled with all types of firearms also. She could shoot the wings off of a housefly without killing it. She is highly skilled in martial arts. She tried to love often. However, the guys would let her down. She would smile at any and everyone with a bubbly personality. Once you got in close, the test would begin. She stayed away from guys that promised her the world often. Sometimes she would give them a chance just to prove a point. The guys would end up not being up to the task. She would make the would-be suitors look like scared little boys. Jade was planning a fun in the sun relaxing yet business trip for the queens. During the meeting, there was a knock at the door. It was Ryan Hunter.

Hunter is an accountant, but of course in reality, he's all geek and nothing else. Ryan stuck his head in the door then stepped in. "I'm here for the "Don't Knock it Till You Try it Event," Ryan says flooded with anxiety.

"I'm not sure what that is," Jade replied.

"Oh ok. Sorry to bother you," he says.

As he prepared to leave, Jade says, "Wait!" in a suspicious voice. She walked up to him and began getting the information on what it was. He let her know it was an event that helped people to think outside of the box during dating.

"Oh ok," she says.

Something in her mentally acute mind told her to try with this guy. Jade grabbed his wrist in a controlling manner and says, "Let's go!"

The doorman found Ryan's name on the list. However, Jade wasn't on the list. "I'm with him. Right Ryan," she says as she stared at him right in his eyes like an optometrist's examining his pupils.

"Oh, Oh Rrright," says Ryan.

This arrangement worked out well because Ryan wasn't a bossy type and he feared trying to talk to attractive, powerful women. By the time he expressed how he felt, it seemed years may pass. Jade liked this because she found a guy that didn't have the slightest desire to control her. As the night passed on, she started to share information with him that she never told anyone. To her, this first meeting seemed like a ten year friendship. She never told him her name. However, she had some of her top hackers and secret agents to get his information instantly.

"Ok Dave. Work it out," says Donique like a mom watching her child playing little league ball.
"Work what out?" David says in confusion.

"Dance silly," Donique says as she chuckles.

"Alright money Mike," says Keisha.

"Just tryin' keep up with you K-quick," says Michael.

"K-quick? I like that," Keisha says.

"You move pretty good for a big guy," says Lena.

"You make me move gorgeous," says Jonathan.

"Ok you gangsta wit it!" says Tasha.

"Well, just call me pretty Tony," Anthony says.

"Okay! You too much!" says Tasha while laughing and nodding.

On the other side of the room, there is some interesting dancing going on. Markita starts stepping. She's dancing like a dude. She's pointing her fist in the air and her index finger. Nathan starts to pick it up and steps with her. "I see you," says Markita.

"Just trying to keep up with the master."

"Oh really," replies Markita.

Jade snaps at Ryan and points to the dance floor. Surely she thought this gesture would make him mad or the male ego come out. She then starts to dance with advanced hip hop dance moves. She starts doing b boy dancing. Then she does choreographed spins and break dances. She has been dancing since she was 5. Ryan watched in awe. He then does a weird little 2 step. Jade looks at him smiling thinking to herself *that will do*.

The music slows down. The guys stand in a state of confusion. The girls know why. So, they initiate a little more. "And where you goin'?" says Donique like the mother of a child trying to sneak off.

David starts stuttering, "Well I…I don't know how to."

Donique cuts him off while he talks, "Just follow me."

David places his hand in her hand. Donique places his hands on her waist.

"What's wrong Mike?" asks Keisha

"I don't really slow dance," says Michael.

"Now you do," says Keisha as she grabs his wrist.

"Well I'm open to new things," says Michael.

Jonathan tries to leave during the slow song, "When it comes to slow songs I'm like a car with bad shocks."

"You aight. I'll work with you. I'll make you like an old school caddy, long but smooth," says Lena.

As he's walking, she steps in front of him and says, "If you try to leave, you'll have a diamond in the back sunroof top with four flat gangsta white walls."

Jonathan replies, "Since you put it that way I'll bag back into the garage." She slow dances counting in his ear softly to help him keep the rhythm.

"Well it's been nice," says Anthony as he starts to walk off.

Tasha stands in front of him with a hand on her hip and an eyebrow arched, "Been nice? It's about to get even better."

Anthony tries to stutter a rebuttal, "Bbbut."

Tasha places her finger on his mouth. "Come on," she says in a soft voice like a mother bidding her little toddler to walk to her.

Markita and Nathan stare at each other in a confused manner as the slow music plays. "So what we gon' do?" replies Markita in her "are you gonna ride or die with me or run like a punk" voice.

Nathan's reply is one that surprises her, "You already know. Aint nothing to it but to do it."

They start dancing slow. "Just relax and ride the beat," says Markita.

These two are completely different stories. However during this dance, they are on the same page.

The music plays on soft and slow. Ryan says in a quick and hasty voice, "I'm gonna sit this out."

Jade says in an extremely demanding tone, "No you're not!"

He repeats, "No really I think I'm".

She grabs his arm as he tries to walk off. She says through her teeth staring in his eyes as if to break him, "No you're not!"

He starts to sigh in a pouting manner.

She then says, "I have spoken".

He sees she means business. This attracts him. They start dancing slow. Ryan starts trembling. He's holding her and dancing like he's scared to touch her. "Don't be shaking while you holding me," she says like a mother would telling her child to stop crying as if they could help it after a whooping.

He gets a little closer, but not as much or as soon as she wants.

She says in an "I won't take any excuses tone", "Stop being a chicken and hold me".

She puts both hands in his back and yanks him close. While they are dancing, she looks around for a second as if to say, "I dare any woman to try it he's mine". Jade knows what she could make happen at the snap of a finger.

The get together is over. Everyone is exiting the floor and standing around talking. "Are we gonna get to see y'all again?" asks Michael.

"Yeah how bout we all exchange numbers," says Keisha.

Everyone gives out numbers.

"We'll see y'all later," says Keisha.

"It's been a pleasure Keisha," says Michael.

"The pleasures all mine," says Keisha as she winks.

"So is that it Nathan?" says Markita.

"Nah!" Nathan replies in a high pitched voice.

They exchange numbers.

Jade grabs Ryan's phone, enters her contact information then calls him saying, "Lock me in."

For her this was an order, and he does as he was told and locks her in.

The guys and girls are talking about the night they had in their respective rooms. "That Michael is alright. He's very respectful," says Keisha.

"Jonathan is big and strong yet gentle," says Donique.

"Anthony is a good boy and got a little hood boy swag to him," says Tasha.

"David is cute and funny. He got smoothness to him too, and he aint over doin it," said Donique.

"So is there gonna be a round 2 ladies?" Keisha asks.

"You know it!" says Lena while pointing and shaking her neck with attitude.

"For sho!" says Tasha looking as if to say "Don't ask stupid questions".

"Shoot! This is gon' be a fifteen round fight," Donique laughs as she makes her statement. All the ladies laugh.

Markita has never really felt this way. She now wants to talk to someone. She makes a call to one of her long time home-girls. "Hello," the caller states.

"Hello Mama," Markita says kind of reluctantly.

"Yes Markita."

"Mama, I need your help," Markita says with little girl bashfulness.
"What you done did now Markita?" she sighs not really wanting to know.

"No. It's not like that Mama."

"Well what is it?" her mother asks trying to get to the bottom.

"I need your advice mama. I met this guy, and he's a real straight edge dude" "You know how I am."

They both laugh.

"Yes I do but baby a real man will not only accept you and your baggage but he will help you unpack. Don't be ashamed of your past. Be open and honest with him and you'll be surprised."

Markita and her mother were always close but separate on certain issues. Her mother is ecstatic that they are talking about this. Never in her wildest dreams had she imagined that her little girl would bring this to her. She always reminded her that she didn't raise a tomboy. She raised a lady. Hours go by and they are laughing. Markita is giggling saying, "Really Mama? That will work."

Her mother replies, "How do you think I hooked your father?"

The boys are all talking. This is like a sports post game film session.

"Keisha is fine, and she's strong but not too much," says Michael.

"Lena is a strong woman too, but she has a gentle side," says Jonathan.

"Tasha is understanding and fun," says Anthony.

"Donique's attitude is real attractive. She's got attitude in the right way, a fun loving way," says David.

Nathan is in unfamiliar territory with Markita, so he decides to call his buddy Smooth. Smooth is a player, a hustler, and all the above. However, no matter how much he knows the game, he gives Nathan the scoop and protects him at all cost. He never gives him game that he cannot handle. He helps to customize the game according to his abilities. Some players are stars and some are role players. Smooth knows this. He saw Nathan get hurt before. Nathan was messing with a suburban chick that was trying to be hood. She told Nathan that he wasn't hood enough and played him.

Nathan went through a dark depression. Smooth never wanted to see this happen again. Smooth answers the phone, "What up Natron?"

"Well Smooth, I met a woman," says Nathan.

"So what's wrong with her?" Smooth asks in his inspection voice.

"Well....?" Nathan says with hesitation.

"C'mon Nate you can't be slick with a can of oil."

"Ok. She's kinda rough around the edges," says Nathan.

"Well you know how that is Nate," says Smooth then continues, "There are two schools of thought. She is rough 'cause she got hurt before or because she wants to be."

"But a woman always has a soft spot."

"This is how you play it. You be Clark Kent. Be this way but really you Superman. Be the kind caring person you are. So, in essence you're not playing because that's who you really are. Show her that there is nothing to protect herself from. That she don't have to use game and that you got her back. Like if she were in the streets you'd be the one to pull out that burna if she needed you to."

"That's deep," says Nathan.

59

Tonight Is the Night

The cruise ship has pulled into a small island. "We have pulled into island. We'll be here for two days. Thank you for traveling festival cruise lines," says the announcer.

The guys and girls meet in the lobby. Both groups stand around without plans. They are talking with very limited conversations. There is absolutely no substance to what they are talking about. They notice a paper with island events listed. "How 'bout jet skiing Donique?" David asked excitedly.

"That sounds like fun," says Donique with her eyes lit up.

"How 'bout Para skiing Keisha?" asked Michael.

"Ok," says Keisha with a "why not?" look on her face.

"I just feel like swimming," says Johnathan.

"Me too," says Lena.

"How 'bout swimming and playing with the Dolphins Tasha?" asked Johnathan

"Just call me flipper," says Tasha happily.

Donique walks up in her bathing suit and catches David staring at her. "You ready?" she asks.

"Ready for what?" he says as his voice cracks as if he was a little boy and man all in one split second.

"Jet skis," she says.

"Oh yeah that is what we came here to do," he says.

She shakes her head and laughs.

The jet skis were gorgeous he had a black and white jet ski that had a shine like the sun hitting water during a bright afternoon. Donique's Jet Ski was pink but looked dangerously fast. David assisted her onto to her jet ski. He was a true gentleman. "Whooo! This is fun!" says Donique as she turned up the throttle on her jet ski.

"Whooa! Yeah it is!" says David nervously as he picked up speed to keep up with Donique.

"Hey, How 'bout you and your girl vs. me and my girl in a jet ski race," says the jet-ski guy. Just as they began to ride a gentleman rode up with his girl friend. They looked like they were true professionals. They had on wet suits as well as water shoes.

David looked on with pure amazement and awe and didn't notice Donique breaking her neck to explain to the guy that they were merely new acquaintances. This shocked him, yet made him feel good. Girls in his past would normally break their neck to make sure that people understand that they were just friends as they would quickly blurt. "Sure! What do you think Donique?" asked David.

"You know how I roll! Let's do it!" she says with confidence.

"I'm ready when you are baby," says the jet-ski girl.

"This will be down and back. Tag team style," says the jet-ski guy.

The professional lady starts the race with a burst of speed and gets out ahead. Donique is losing by a small margin. She's losing literally about an inch looking upset. "That's alright. Keep coming! Keep coming!" says David. This makes Donique feel good because she is self-driven because she had to be. No one, especially her man, encouraged her. Donique tags David by passing him. He has to pick up the slack. "Come on Dave. You can do it!" says Donique. Her encouragement was a verbal performance enhancing supplement to him.

He cranked the throttle back with all his might and had laser-beam focus on the finish line. As they approach the home stretch they keep exchanging the lead. At the last minute, David wins by a nose

"Ordinarily I don't talk like this, but that's wassup!" says David. Donique cocks her head back in shock. This sent a tingling sensation through her. She was thinking *Oh baby*!

"David, I didn't know you had it in you," says Donique.

David felt like one of the x-men that had just discovered his mutant power for the first time.

Johnathan was stuck without a lead in to talk to Lena. He was like a bad CD with songs in between the hit tracks.

"So how long have you been swimming?" asked Johnathan.

"Since I was four," says Lena. As she answered his question, she saw his eyes wonder, checking her out.

Jonathan says in amazement, "Four? I still need to use water wings. No, I'm just kidding."

Lena began laughing, "You need to quit!"

"Ok let's race to that spot," Johnathan says.

"Ok," says Lena without an ounce of hesitation.

"She says I'll call it. Ready set go" she says as she pushes him out of the way. Lena gets ahead of Jonathan. Jonathan is getting tired and is gasping for air each time. Lap for lap Johnathan gasps for air then catches up. Jonathan just beats her by a finger tip. Jonathan gasps, "Whoo!"

"So what do you think?" Lena asked.

"You looked great! And your swimming was good too. You swim pretty girl. I mean pretty good," he says as he gives her a playful look.

"It's always the shy ones! I'm gon' have to watch you," says Lena.

She was laughing so hard that she felt a small cramp in her side.

Tasha and Anthony walk down a circular stairway that leads into the dolphin tank. It's all surrounded by underwater foliage. There are rocks, life   rafts, there are written fun facts on plaques about dolphins.

Tasha and Anthony are talking with the dolphin trainer. "Feed them a fish first," says the trainer.

Tasha drops a fish in dolphin's mouth. "Ooh!" she says.

Anthony pats the dolphin hands and feeds it a fish. "Hi," he says.

Tasha holds on to the dolphin and swims, "Whoo hoo!"

Anthony mimicking Will Smith in Independence Day, "I have got to get me one of these!"

"You crazy!" she says laughing.

"Thought you'd like that."

They are now out of the water Tasha and Anthony begin to talk. "These dolphins are fun and playful," says Tasha.

"They remind me of someone," Jonathan says then winks.

"Aww that's sweet," says Tasha.

Michael and Keisha are about to Para-ski. As Keisha walks up, Michael is staring. He's trying not to, but he can't stop. "Whoa that looks exciting," says Michael.

"Yeah and scary," says Keisha.

"I wasn't talking about the skiing," Keisha's mouth drops wide open, "You dirty little dog you. You're so sneaky." She gently taps him on his arm.

She is amazed. She never ever was watched like this by Chris. He was too busy watching all things ESPN. She felt like a little girl that was all dolled up for Sunday school and being told she was pretty. She knew this was non-predatory. "

"Ok next," says the instructor.

"Ladies first," says Michael. He's trying to give off the idea of being polite to really mask his fear.

Keisha knows what game he's playing.

"You something else," she replies.

The boat takes off. Keisha screams and laughs. Michael looks on laughing. "Go head Keisha," he yells as he laughs. She is doing gymnastic moves. She's splitting her legs. She's holding on with one hand. It looks like a water version of the x games.

The boat pulls up, and it is now Michael's turn. "Next," the instructor says.

She gets off the boat looking kind of tired and relieved. Then, she gets her second wind with a super villain look. "Now I get to laugh," Keisha says with revenge and retaliation in her eyes.

The boat speeds off really fast. Michael begins to talk to the driver, "Maybe we can reconsider".

The driver looks at him and laughs. Keisha shakes her head "no" and says, "Un Un. Hit it driver!"

The driver does just as she says and accelerates to full speed in sixty seconds.

"You aint right!" Michael yells at Keisha with his eyes wide open. "Whoa! Ahh! This is too much fun!" He screams.

The boat pulls up and stops. Michael's ride is over. Michael sighs and begins to talk out of breath,

"Phew! That was fun."

"You screamed louder than I did," Keisha says.

"I did and at a higher pitch," Michael says as they both roar in laughter together.

Markita and Nate are in for the time of their lives; Fun and Games at the Islands. This is a kind of an amusement park on the island. "Let's get on the atomic slide Nathan," says Markita.

"I don't know."

"Stop being a punk and C'mon," she says forcefully, but Nathan understands it's her way of showing affection.

"Oh, ok," replies Nathan, "However, we have to slide down facing forward."

"No, no, no!" Markita replies.

"Markita what kind of food does Church's serve?'' Nathan asks and giggles.

"You no what...?" she replies after she gets what he's asking.

They get on the slide and he notices her in that way. He looks like a construction working watching a woman coming down the sidewalk toward the next site.

"M-Markita is that a tattoo on your thigh?"

"Yes you nut!" She feels attractive.

He notices her athletic upper body and muscular legs. He's looking as if he's lightheaded and starts shaking his head and grabbing his temples.

"Are you alright," she asks to kind of snap him back into consciousness.

"Never better," he says jumping his eyebrows up and down.

She walks up the slide shaking her head and laughing. They slide down the slide screaming and laughing having fun, (Describe this fun) after the ride is over, they laugh together. "Ordinarily you think of nose plugs when you swim."

"In your case, I needed earplugs. How loud did you scream on the way down?" Markita replied laughing.

"I know you aint talking Ms. Tough woman. You screamed like a person in the suburbs hearing gun fire," says Nathan.

Markita laughed so hysterically that she fell down because this type of joke was a gap-bridger for her.

They later play games at the carnival. Nathan decides to play the game when you hit the hammer and ring the bell. "Step right up," says the game guy. Nathan takes a deep breath. "C'mon daddy," Markita says.

Nathan thinks *daddy?* All of a sudden he feels a rush of testosterone and adrenaline he never knew he had. Ding! Then he hits it again three times: Ding! Ding! Ding! He gives her a stuffed animal. "Yeah," she shouts.

"Couldn't have done it without my ride or die," Nathan says as he winks at her. This statement made Markita feel a case of the helium heart, of all the people to say this to her.

The girls and guys meet at the restaurant. "So where we gonna sit?" asks Michael.

"I don't know," replies Keisha.

"David and I want to sit by the window," Donique says with implication in her voice.

"We do?" asks David looking confused.

Donique jumps her eyebrows and snatches his wrist, "Yeah we do."

David begins stuttering, "Yyyeah! Whoa!" He feels like a little boy being dragged by his mother through a grocery store.

"That booth looks nice and comfortable. What do you think Lena?"

"Real comfortable," Lena says as she winks.

"Well let's get going," Jonathan says is an adventurous sea captain voice.

"How 'bout the patio, so we can get some fresh air and cool breeze?" Anthony asks.

"Just call me Scarlett. I'm ready to be gone with the wind," says Tasha.

Michael and Keisha look at each other and laugh. "How 'bout that spot by the plant," asks Michael.

"Ok," says Keisha.

Michael begins to attempt to freestyle, "Ok then let's change the scenery, picture us sitting next to the greenery. Nah! Just playin'"

Keisha doesn't care about the quality of the rhyme. She is just basking in the ambiance of the moment. "You need to quit," she says while giggling. One-on-one conversations begin.

"This is nice. I like this place is nice," says Donique.

"I agree," says David.

"I've never really dated a guy like you before," says Donique.

"Like me? What do you mean?" David asks.

"You know. Reading books and watching Star Wars."

"It's ok to say geek or nerd?" says David.

Donique giggles, "Ok."

"I've never dated someone outspoken, who speaks with confidence and says how she feels," David says in a returning synopsis.
"It's ok to say hood," Donique says.

"Well..." David says as he laughs.

David and Donique both laugh.

"This is a nice experience and interesting change," says Jonathan.

"Change?" she asks because she's lost.

"Why Yes. Talking to an exciting woman like you. Ordinarily, I'd be like a tall lonely tree in the middle of the park while everyone is playing," he says.

"You're a good change too. Ordinarily the guys I date are...well you wouldn't be interested," Lena says.

"Humor me," Jonathan replies.

"This is a great view," says Tasha.

"The patio view is nice also," says Anthony.

Tasha starts blushing, "I like to see happy people."

"The amazing part is that they have lives and people to go home to also. So tell me what makes you happy Tasha? I like being able to have intelligent conversations," he says.

Tasha is amazed that anyone wants to even know what makes her happy. It's a lost art to not just have to ask "yes" and "no" or closed-ended questions.

"Yeah, it feels good to be able to have an adult conversation."

"It does," Anthony replies.

"This is real fancy," says Michael.

"Yeah it is, but I don't have to have all of this."

"Oh really? Keisha I'm impressed," says Michael.

"Impressed how?" Keisha asks.

"You are not a shallow person. You see that there is more to life than buying and receiving gifts. More important it's the quality of life and conversation."

"I agree," says Keisha.

There's another dinner date that's going on. It's Nathan and Markita.

"Mmm! Mmm!Mmm! I haven't eaten like this in a while," says Markita. She is used to the jailhouse cuisine or cheap microwave meals. She is cleaning the

72

plates and the bones. Nathan tries not to notice, but he can't help it. It may sound weird, but he likes to see a female that doesn't mind being herself around him. Nathan says inside of himself *No empty holes or dead space. Start talking.* "So what is Markita's type of man?" Nathan asks. Markita is not used to questions unless they are from detectives or law enforcement officials but something inside of her tells her that she can trust this guy. "Well, believe it or not, I like intelligent conversation," she says as if it is hard for her even to believe.

"Oh ok. I agree. I believe that I can go out on a limb and say that we both have probably taken baths that were deeper than some of our love interests."

"Well…." she says and laughs so does he.

As they walk down the beach at night, there is a violinist. Nathan whispers to him. He plays <u>Pretty Brown Eyes</u> by Mint Condition. She smiles and thinks *Acting all innocent. He needs to quit.*

Ryan hears a knock at the door of his hotel room. He opens the door to see a NFL sized muscular man dressed in secret service attire. He has on an all black suit with sunglasses. He throws a long dry cleaning bag to Ryan. There is a note attached. The note reads "put this on immediately". As soon as he gets dressed into this really expensive tuxedo, he hears a knock again. It's the same secret service looking gentleman, "Follow me." He follows the gentleman. The man walks him outside to a black Chrysler 300 limo. As Ryan gets

73

closer, the back window rolls down. It's Jade Frost, "Are you just gonna stare at me or are you going to get in?"

He steps in timidly and is amazed, looking at the velvet plush interior of the limo as well as the refrigerator and television inside. He looks down and sees Jade's open toed bedazzled shoes. There are jewels on this high heeled stiletto. He also notices the split in her gown. Her hair is bouncing yet behaving. The earrings that she has in her ears are worth a whole year's worth of his salary. Her dress is metallic sky blue. Her fingernails and toenails are painted the same color. She has a hint of sparkling sky blue eye shadow. Her lips look kiss ably moist. She catches him staring. He shakes his head trying to play it off, "So where are we going?" "That's classified information," Jade replies and winks.

They get to a fancy tall ivory building. They get into the ballroom. There is a chandelier that is hanging that looks like it has all of Jared Jewelers' diamonds in it. There are very rich and important people at this function. Jade and Ryan begin to talk. "So what do you do Ryan?" Jade asks with a look of deep investigation and interest in her eyes.

Ryan looks left to right and replies, "I'm an accountant and financial advisor."

Jade is thinking *got him*. All her previous lovers would promise to take care of her but would irresponsibly forget to pay bills on time and waste lots of money. His statement confirmed that this would not be the case.

"So what do you do ma'am?" he asked.

"Please call me Jade," she says. Up until this point she never told him her name. She wanted to keep the mystery game fun factor in this fling. "Well I run a dating service," she says trying to not fully reveal it.
　　Ryan jumped in very excited and says, "Wow! That's why I...." he stopped realizing that his words are now critical. Jade knew why he was here. However, she decided that he was hers now.

They all gather in front of restaurant. Dinner is now over. They are now setting up after dinner activities. They are all unique yet intriguing activities.

Donique and David watch Star Wars. David knocks on the door timidly. Donique answers the door. David is filled with excitement that he feels as if he can barely compose himself. She's wearing a little white girly t-shirt with a big black outlined picture of a storm trooper in the center. She's wearing black open-toed tights. Her toe nails and fingernails are alternated with one nail black and another white. She has storm trooper decals on the nails. On the white nail she has black storm trooper head logo. On the black she has white print and trimmed Darth Vader. David is in awe, "Star Wars has never looked this good! Wow." He then gives a detailed play by play analysis, "White black, white black fingernails and feet. He stops and stares at her feet saying, "Those are the prettiest feet I've ever seen...Oh, I hope you don't think that I'm weird." She says, "it's ok." She is overwhelmed. She has never had a man pay that close attention to her. Donique holds onto that thought about his little foot fetish. She will use this as a weapon later. He stands there dazed and confused. She says, "Come on." "Oh yeah," he replies.

She catches him checking her out. She loves every minute of it. He's fumbling with the DVD's. He's so nervous. Finally he puts the DVD in. She says, "I have a surprise treat for the movie." She has Star Wars fruit snacks. In a 10 year old voice he shouts, "Oh boy!" She feels great that someone appreciates something so small. David sits down on the couch. He's going through his internal safety manual. *Don't sit too close. Be respectful*, he says inside. Donique scoots next to him. She puts her open hand next to his leg. He goes through a state of confusion. David hears the inner David shouting, "Hold her hand stupid!" He thinks *well here goes nothing*. Slowly but surely he holds her hand. She clasps her hand closed to show she welcomes and wants it.

As the movie progresses, so does she. She now moans and shifts her weight, lays her left shoulder against him, and her head on his heart. She feels it beating fast. He asks, "Are you ok? Do you have enough room?" She says, "I'm fine baby." He's stunned. He's thinks *Baby?* He then squeezes her with his right arm. The sweet smelling aroma of her Ed Hardy perfume has him going crazy. Donique is going crazy over his Drakkar. He loves the feeling of her soft perfectly permed hair.

As the night progresses, so does Donique. She methodically and meticulously remembers his little foot fetish, so she does the unthinkable. She rubs her foot up and down his bare shin. He's driven so crazy that he digs his nails into the seat cushions. "That Darth Vader is space Hood!" Donique says.

"You're right."
"So what's it like in your world? As far as romance is concerned?" she asks

"Remember warp speed?" he says and then laughs, "No I'm playing. Well, I'm a little shy with women. How 'bout you?" he asks.

"Well I have had from my most recent previous romance a man that didn't appreciate me," she says sighing.

"Well one thing I can tell you about dating a geek. We'll appreciate you. To me, this is like dating a supermodel or someone from a magazine cover. I'm acting calm but I'm really throwing a fit inside."

"That is so sweet," Donique says

Tasha and Anthony are on the deck of the ship. Tasha is holding onto the rail. She signals Anthony to get closer. When he does, she reaches backwards and grabs his wrists and pulls him forward so that he is hugging her from behind around the waist. He's very scared at first then he puts his chin on her shoulder and presses his face against hers.

"I bet you break a lot of hearts," Anthony says.

"More like get mine broken," She says.

"What do you mean?" Anthony asks sincerely.

"My ex wanted to watch TV more than me," She says.

"I personally could live with just using a DVR. A guy like me, you know a nerd, I would treat you like a computer program. I would make sure I input all the right codes to make you happy and run smooth," Anthony says.

"You won't need to hack. I'll give you the password," says Tasha playing along.

Lena and Jonathan are sitting in an empty lounge room. "I don't know what your life is like with the opposite sex. Mine isn't really that good."

"Maybe you haven't met the right guy yet. Why I'd...," says Jonathan and then pauses.

"You'd what?" asks Lena.

"Nah. It'll sound cheesy," Jonathan says.

Lena with one eyebrow raised, "Humor me."

Jonathan realizes his own words "humor me"

were used against him. *Excellent strategy* he thought. "I'd treat you like a math equation. The same enthusiasm I have to solve it. I would use that on you to find the answer to your happiness," says Jonathan.

Lena with a surprised look on her face replies, "Well, I certainly would let you solve for Y!"

"So is there a leading lady or friend?" Keisha asked.

"No. How 'bout you?" says Michael.

"Nah we broke it off. He just didn't care," Keisha says.

Michael says with an uncharacteristic confidence, "Well rest assured, if you date a guy like me, you know a nerd, geek, smart guy, I would treat you like a college course. I would take notes on what you want Professor Keisha. I want to pass 'Intro to loving you'," he says.

Keisha jumped back in amazement. "Well, you'd be on the Dean's list," she replied.

The boys and girls are coming back from their long dates. The girls know if there is going be any actions from their much more shy boys; they will have to encourage them a little bit.

"Well David this was nice I heard you say earlier that you were having a fit yet. I got something that will give you a fit," Donique steps forward.

David begins talking frantically and stuttering, "Are you about do what I think you are? What about the ramifications?" His hands tremble. He gets a lump in his throat. A mild sweat breaks on his forehead.

"I got your ramifications right here," She says. She snatches his arms throws his arms around her waist.

David says, "Oh no, I've seen this move before."

She kisses him passionately. As they lock up, Donique feels his grip around her waist get tighter and tighter. She feels the bulge of his arms, forearms, and chest muscles. While he kisses her, he whispers things like "you deserve the finer things in life" and "You're worth it". She's so driven with passion that the real her comes out. She thinks, *if this boy say one more sweet thing. I'm gone attack him! I wish he would try to leave me! I'd tear up all them Star Wars dolls, light sabers and e'rthing!*

"Whoo!" David sighs, "Oops. Did I say that aloud?" he asks.

"Yes you did," Donique says then waives daintily, "Goodbye my Jedi."

"Hey Anthony this has been so nice," says Tasha.

"I agree," says Anthony.

"I got another computer language I want to show

you," He starts naming off a list, Visual C#, Visual Basic, MaxScript and many more. Still clueless, he keeps going down the list. She keeps shaking her head "no" and starts kissing him while he speaks. He kisses her passionately on the lips then gently raises her neck, kisses her, and whispers, "I would love to hear your dreams and share mine with you." This statement causes her to think inside, *I've had it! This little geek is about to get his RAM, ROM, or whatever burnt out.* Anthony shakes head and blinks, "I think my system just crashed."

"Wow Jonathan I had a great time!" Lena says.

"Me too," Jonathan replies.

"Remember when we talked about math?" Lena asks.

"Yeah I do," he replies.

"Well I got an equation for you. M+Y = MNU. Wanna solve for Y?" Lena asks as she slides close.

"I'm beginning to think this isn't math were talking about," Jonathan says.

"I'm your variable," she says then grabs him.

He chimes in and says, "I-I-I never..."

She realizes that he is trying to say that he has never kissed a woman before. His statement only digs him in a worse hole. His inexperience is cute to her and makes her feel more aggressive. She talks him through it ironically like a math teacher helping him through an equation. He starts to suck and savor her lips and give her tongue. She feels like a coach watching her star athlete. "Now I know that math is my favorite subject," Jonathan says.

"I enjoyed myself Keisha," Michael says.

"Me too," Keisha says. She stares at him with desire. Now he sees how it feels to be stared at. "Remember when we talked about college?" she asks.
"Yes," he says as he looks around wondering where this is going.

"Well I was thinking I want you to get an 'A' in "Intro to loving me," she says.

"Ok," he says.

"Well, I'll need you to do an extra credit project," says Keisha.

She grabs him by his shirt and kisses him. As they kiss, he holds her and rubs her back. He whispers to her, "You deserve more, not just money, but quality of life". She feels weak like she is about to cry because this is what she was trying to tell Chris, a man that she was in a relationship with for years and here's a guy that's known her for only a short time, and he's aware of this already. "I can't wait for the upper level courses!" says Michael.

Things are heating up with Nathan and Markita now. Nathan knocks on the door as if he's an outsider visiting an unfamiliar housing project. Markita answers the door. "What up?" she says as she answers the door.

"Hey how you doing?" Nathan asks.

She says, "I got a surprise snack for us."

They sit down, and she presents him with Ramen noodles and Doritos mixed together with cheese. She starts to get kind of aggressive in a good way. She says, "Let me show you how to eat them," she walks up behind him, "Tilt your head back a little and relax."
He opens his mouth and she drops them in letting him get a touch of her index and pointer finger against his lips. They both start to enjoy their meal and start talking.

"So Markita lets talk about your past."

She gets a little nervous, but she remembers what her mother tells her.

"Well, let me go first. You started last time," says Nathan, "I'm a therapist, a Licensed Professional Counselor. I've always lived life in a confined area. I didn't really go out much. I'm not a social butterfly."

Markita is especially relating to the confined area, but of course it's because she was in prison. "So enough about me. Let's talk about you," asked Nathan.

"I'm gonna be honest. I grew up on the west side of town. My dad wasn't around much. I grew up a tomboy. I'm gonna keep it 100 with you. I've been in and out of prison," she was expecting a sigh, flinch, or something. However, Nathan didn't budge. "Did you hear what I just said?"

"Yes," replied Nathan, "I knew."

"How'd you know?" she asked.

"You fed me breaks," he replied.

"How do you know about breaks?" she asked.
"I've had family as well as clients that were in the system. As a matter of fact, one of my closest advisors was there," he stated.

"That doesn't bother you?" she asked.

"As long as you're cool, so am I."

They began to share more of their past. He sat attentively, looked, and was genuinely interested in all her very words. He then cracked a joke that made her laugh hard. He asked, "Do want to see my criminal record?" She looked confused. "Here it is," he laid down a blank sheet of paper on the table. She laughed till she cried. She says, "I've got something I want to show you." She came out of the room with a black briefcase. Nathan was wondering is this a 9 millimeter or 380 in this case. She opened the case. "Pow!" she says. It was a chess board. "You don't want none!" she says. "Oh quite

84

the contrary," stated Nathan.

They set up the board, and a few minutes maybe even seconds later, Markita stated, "Check mate!" She had beaten him in 4 moves. "How did you?" Nathan asked in amazement.

"I had a lot of time to devote to the game," she laughed.

"I still can't believe it," Nathan says.

She says, "I've got one more thing to show you."

She went back to the room. This next surprise would prove to be scarier than any gun or anything that Nathan could imagine. She walked out of the room with silver earth tone toe nail polish and fingernail polish, a gray tank-top, and gray plaid shorts. She had a slight silver smoky eye with a dash of eye shadow. She had silver lip-stick. Nathan was very unfamiliar with this type of situation. "What do you think?" she asked.

"Call the cops it has to be at least a felony to look that good," Nathan replied. She blushes. "I'll be back," he says. He runs to the phone in the room to try to call someone. "Hello, Hello!" then he grabs the cord and sees that it has been cut. Markita is standing over him in the doorway with scissors snipping them open and closed. He grabs his cell phone, "Hello, Hello". With his battery in her hand, she asks, "Looking for this?" She then throws the battery and scissors aside. She has him cornered. She says, "Fresh meat!" He screams like a teenage girl that has found out that she is going on a date with the quarterback of the football team. He realizes that he is trapped then says, "I don't do victim well. I tried to be nice to you but you don't understand that! I've had it! I'm about to kick it to you hood!" he says, "I'm gonna make you my cell mate!" This was pleasurably scary to her. She tried to keep it out, but love is now breaking and entering.

He scoops her up like a groom carrying his bride over the threshold. They land on the couch. He has one arm under her back, and the other underneath her thighs. He's holding her like a baby. He's kissing her passionately. She's moaning in a womanly manner. He pulls back and says, "Your record is expunged with me. I'm gonna be your bell boy and help you unpack your baggage." At that very moment, she remembered what her mother said.

He's running his fingers through her hair and holding her tight. She's flushed with endorphins. She loves the feeling of the manly force he displays on her. She feels like something she has never felt before. She feels like she is sky diving, drag racing, competing in an Olympic event. Above all things she feels like a woman. Nathan feels an inner thug go through him that he has never felt before. Inside he says *this is my woman. I'll give her more bands than black college football games.* This wasn't like him. After this, he held her. She probably enjoyed this more than anything. She felt like, for once in her life, a man wasn't trying to get over on her or look down on her because she was a woman. Also she felt like this man loved the skin that he's in and didn't have to compete with or be jealous of her nor she of him.

Jade signaled her driver to pop the trunk of the limo. There was a bathing suit in there for her and relaxed island clothes for him. They pull up to an island apparel clothing store. Jade snaps her finger and the clerk assisted them to the dressing room. The clerk asked no questions because Jade had tipped her beyond her wildest dreams earlier when she purchased these outfits that were in the trunk.

They walked on the beach. The moon cast its bluish hue onto the sand and the ocean. Jade grabbed his hand as they discussed romance and finance. "So Jade is there a Mr. Powerful in your life?" asked Ryan. Jade laughed hysterically. "What's so funny?" he asked seriously.

"All the men that I've ever dated tried to control me. That ain't happening no more!" she says then asks, "How 'bout you?"

"Ironically, I had the same situation. They tried to control me, but when I decided to rebel, they ran," he says.

They both stopped talking and took a second to meditate. Jade knew it was time to move in for the kill. "It's time for some Frost on the beach," Jade says.

Ryan didn't have a clue what she was talking about. He took this literal. She stared into his eyes and says, "I heard that it is magical to kiss on the beach under the moonlight." By the time he was even thinking to reply, she started kissing him passionately. She put both arms around his neck. He used both of his hands to palm her waist. She loved this feeling and couldn't believe that for once that the strong grip of loving control had grabbed her, and she freely wanted to surrender. Ryan felt like an executive instead of a mere accountant. This sent a sudden surge of power all through him. He dealt with all kinds of rich tycoons, handled accounts for them, and knew the agony of the crown. As they kissed and held each other, the stars sparkled like diamonds in the sky as if to cheer them on.

All the girls are driven crazy by the kisses of the men. The men sighed and hugged them after the kisses were over. The ladies had that feeling of mothers that soothed a baby's troubled heart. This story turned out to be a contradictory twist to things. The damsels in distress decided to save the princes'. The comic book heroes were rescued by their amazons or wonder women. This truly was an inverse variation. Parts of the psyche that had not been activated were now being tickled with attraction.

Michael and his boys are in their room. Keisha and the girls are in theirs.

"So how was everybody's night?" Keisha asks.

"It was good," says Tasha with a blank look on her face.

"Good," says Lena quickly.

"Donique, how was your night?" Keisha asked.

"It was aight," Donique

Keisha didn't buy this at all, "Ooh you need to quit."

Lena jumped in. She knew Donique like the back of her hand, "Don't tell me you kissed him?"

"You didn't?!" Tasha says.

"I did. He started talking 'bout Star Wars, so I kissed him and took him to another galaxy," Donique replied with a "no shame or regard for human life" look on her face. All the girls screamed and stomped their feet.

"Lena?" Keisha asked.

"Well Jonathan was talking 'bout him loving me like math, so I gave him the formula to solve this equation. I kissed him," says Lena shaking her neck with attitude.

"I know she didn't!" Tash says.

Keisha now interrogates Tasha, "Come on. Spill it Tasha!"

"Anthony started talking 'bout me and a computer, so I kissed him and made his system freeze.

He had to reboot," Tasha says.

"Hold up! Wait a minute! Wait a minute! Keisha up here questioning us. What about you?" Lena asked

"You know us. You know," says Keisha feeling trapped.

"Nah we don't know?" says Donique quickly firing.

"Michael compared me to a college course. Brotha 'bout to get his degree. I kissed him," says Keisha. All of the girls erupt in laughter and hi fives.

"So how y'all doing? Have fun?" Michael asked. David replies with a big grin on his face, "Yeah."

Anthony begins looking around smiling, "You know it."

Jonathan replies nodding a smiling with amazement, "Ohh yeah!"

Michael is trying to get to the bottom of it all, "Dave what's going on? I haven't seen you smile that big since they released the collector's edition of Star Wars."

"Well, we talked about dating a guy like me being unusual and things like that," David replied withholding pertinent information.

"You kissed her didn't you?" Michael says.

David laughs out real loud, "Something like that." Anthony points emphatically while pointing, "Yeah he did!"

Jonathan falls back on bed laughing, "She snatched me up and kissed me."

"What are you laughing at Jonathan? How 'bout you?" David says.

"Well, we talked about math, but she wanted to skip the steps and she solved for x and y. She kissed me," Jonathan says then continues, "So Anthony, what's up?" You pointing out my sins." Jonathan laughs.

"Well, Tasha and I were discussing computers. She couldn't wait for the system to get booted up, or the windows to load up, so Lena kissed me," says Anthony owning up to the allegations.

"So how 'bout our fearless leader Michael?" Anthony asks.

"Don't worry about me," Michael says as he laughs.

"Aw man," says David.

"Oh ok," says Jonathan.

"Nah I'm just playing. Keisha and I were talking about college. She took me to grad school. We kissed. It was more her pulling me in.

How Well Do You Know Me?

Dr. Hampton sets up a game so that each set of couples can prove how well they know their mates. It really is a way to bring each couple even closer. "Hey everyone, we're going to play a game. We're going to see how well you know your new friends. We need a group of 8 over here and a group of 8 over there," says Dr. Hampton (Boys and girl volunteer) then continues, "This game is going to be in the format to where I'll call up a team member individually to answer questions from the survey in the packet you originally received. The team with the most points at the end of the 3 rounds will win," says Dr. Hampton.

(Round 1 Donique versus Brittany)

"Brittany, what's your partner's favorite movie?" Dr Hampton asks as she reads the card.

"Rocky," says Brittany.

Dr. Hampton pauses, "That's correct."

"Yes!" Brittany says and pumps her fist

"Donique, what is your partner's favorite movie?" Dr. Hampton says.

"Ooh I know this. Star Wars!" Heeey! Heeey! Heeey!" says Donique.

"That's correct," says Dr. Hampton.

Donique runs back into the group hi-fiving.

"You are so smart! You are so smart!" says David. Donique is truly flattered by this commit. She's very happy to hear a genius calling her smart.
(David vs. Alan)

"It's now time for multiple choices. How does Donique consider herself? a) Outgoing, b) shy or c) in between," says Dr Hampton.

"Outgoing," says David

Dr. Hampton says, "That answer is correct."

David shakes hands with the guys, other girls then hugs Donique. David is looking at Donique right in her eyes, "Learned from the best," he winks at her.

"Alan, what is your partner's character type? a) outgoing, b) shy or c) in between?" Dr. Hampton asks.

"I'll say shy," Alan says.

"That's correct," says Dr. Hampton.
(Keisha vs. Kaitlin)

"Kaitlin, what is your partner's favorite subject in school?"

Kaitlin reluctantly says, "Math?"

"Correct," Dr. Hampton replies.

"Keisha what is your partner's favorite subject in school?" asks Dr. Hampton;

"Psychology," says Keisha.

"That answer... Is correct," says Dr. Hampton. (Jenny vs. Tasha)

"Jenny what is your partner's favorite hobby?" asks Dr. Hampton.

"Working out," says Jenn.

"That is correct," say Dr. Hampton.

"Tasha what is your partner's favorite hobby?" asks Dr. Hampton.

"Computers," says Tasha.

"Correct," says Dr. Hampton. (Anthony vs. Chuck)

"Chuck what's a big turn off for your partner with the opposite sex?" asks Dr. Hampton.

"Lack of eye contact," Chuck replies.

"Correct," says Dr. Hampton.

"Anthony your partner's turn offs?"

"Guys who don't like to talk," says Anthony.

"Correct," says Dr. Hampton.
Anthony stands, poses, and everyone laughs.
(Lena vs. Tina)

Dr. Hampton asks, "Lena what's your partner's nickname?"

Lena replies, "Big John Stud."

The crowd laughs.

Dr. Hampton replies, "Correct."

Dr. Hampton leads into the next question, "Tina, What is your partner's nickname?"

Tina replies, "The Iceman."

The crowd laughs again.

Dr. Hampton replies, "And you're correct."
(John vs. Jake)

Dr. Hampton asks Jake, "What does your partner do to relieve stress?"

Jake replies, "Jogs"

Dr. Hampton fires back, "Correct."

Dr. Hampton asks Jonathan, "What does your partner do to relieve stress?"

Jonathan responds, "Talks with friends."
96

Dr. Hampton replies, "I'm sorry, that is incorrect."

Jonathan walks away swinging his fists in anger. Jonathan is a huge Jeopardy fan, so for him to miss this question is a slap in the face. Lena gives him a sympathetic smile, pats him on the back, and says, "That's alright baby. Sometimes in Jeopardy you have to lose points to gain." This is a great shock. He never told her that he's a Jeopardy fan.

Dr. Hampton says with excitement in her voice, "Were now in Round 2. Points are double!"

Each individual is raising their hand answering some right and then some wrong answers.
Dr. Hampton says with suspense in her voice, "The last team got a wrong answer. This last question will be for the game. Contestants will choose their spokesman."

Michael takes the leadership role and says, "Jonathan get in there."

Jonathan is still feeling the dejection of his last minor failure and says, "I can't."

Michael merely says, "Remember Yoda?"

Jonathan looks up with a razor sharp acuity and focus then says, "Ok."

Dr. Hampton asks, "Who is your partner's favorite Old school group?"

97

Jonathan looks down like there's no hope. Dr. Hampton says with compassion, "We need an answer Jonathan."

Jonathan answers the question while closing his eyes, "The Ohio Players."

Dr. Hampton says, "That's correct team A!!! You each win $1000 in cash!"

Lena runs over to him and says, "Told you it would be alright." She then kisses him on the lips.

Jonathan says, "Thank you sweetheart."

After the contest, Dr. Hampton is confronted by an intern, "Doc, I've read all your books and reviewed all your research. I want to be your intern." This young man is a doctoral student. He's had nothing but a 4.0 G.P.A since he was in undergrad. He was in the clinical research program. Dr. Hampton accepts the offer. However, her intentions aren't good. She calculates the year that the intern got out of school and realizes she's a little older. Inside, she starts the therapeutic technique of self talk. "Well, I certainly do believe in my own product," she says.

The intern looks like a body builder in a suit and tie. His suit is tailor made fitting each contour of his muscular form. One day the intern says, "Well Doc, I've graded all the tests and all the homework. It looks like all my work is done."

She looks at him with desire and says, "Not all your work." She sits on the front of her desk, takes off her glasses, and lets her hair down.

The intern says, "Oh no!"

She says, "Oh yes."

He stands still frozen with fear. He starts to name off psychological complexes and situations.

She says, "Don't give me that theoretical crap!"

She shoves him into the file cabinet. His back is against the front of the file cabinet. He has no escape. He tries to name codes then says, "What about the no fraternizing with intern's clause?" She grabs him in an attempt to kiss him. He moves from in front of the file cabinet, backing towards the wall. Once his back touches the wall, he shouts, "Stop Dr Hampton Stop!" She's been practicing therapy for 5 years she knows in this case, "no" really means "yes". She kisses him. His back starts to slide down the wall. He throws the experiment results chart into the air as paperwork flies everywhere. He then confesses, "I knew you needed this. I'm the cure for your hero complex."

"My little smart intern. You've out psyched your mentor," she says.

"Don't worry. I'll always learn and look up to you boss lady."

That feeling of a man not ashamed to be in submission without feeling like he wasn't as smart or threatened drove the psychologist nuts. How ironic? The doctor felt something that she hadn't felt in a long time. She felt the feeling of being allowed to feel, being vulnerable, and not having to shield her feelings to cure others. Inside she says *this must be what my clients that are made whole again feel like. This is Love Therapy.*

The Conflict

Michael, his boys, and Keisha, and her girls are in for a surprise. The boys and girls are celebrating their win and Malik, Chris, Tyrone, and Lance show up, as well as the female nemesis' Asia, Shawn, Janelle, and Janine.

Michael says to Keisha, "Yeah I can't believe it."

"Yeah me neither," Keisha says.

Asia walks up fast and with force in her voice, "I know you ain't talking to my man!" she says.

Asia is gorgeous. She looks like Kimora Simmons. She has tattoos on her back foot and arms. She has the latest shoes and purses. Wet Seal, Forever 21, and other stores gain billions in taxes from her alone. She had an issue with Michael, because in her words, he was not ghetto enough. She was used to guys in the streets that would hit her and call her disrespectful names. To her, that type of treatment was normal.

Keisha immediately wanting an explanation turns and asks in a demanding tone, "Michael, you know her?"

Michael starts to explain, "Yeah I…….."

Asia jumps in immediately, "Tell her about us."

Keisha asks, "Us? You know what." She walks

off stomping and breathing in a tantrum.

Donique smiles and tells David, "You did great!"

David replies, "Thanks. I take after you." David met Shawn while he was in college. He was there for her as a friend. She was in a long relationship, in and out for 9 years. He was only given the title of a friend. After she would break up with her boyfriend, she would then start acting as if she wanted a relationship with him. They would study together and take classes together, then as soon as the ex started showing signs of getting back together, she would break the news to him that they would need to not see each other. She would eventually call him back again. In the meantime, there were cheerleaders, sorority girls, and women's college athletes that were trying to talk to him. However, he turned them all down because somewhere he hoped that she would give him the chance. He even graduated college, came back from Georgia to return to Ohio to give love a try with her. After he came back to Ohio, she later informed him that she wanted to be in a relationship. Her plan backfired. Her ex ended up getting sick of the competition with David. He broke up with her for good and is now happily married. She went to the military and served her time. While she was away, all she could do is think of what could've been. Shawn jumps in arrogantly, "Let me guess Star Wars? He used that on me."

Donique asks with attitude, "David, who is this?"

David tries to explain, "I used to talk to her as friends."

Donique jumps in squinting in angry disgust, "Friends?! I know what that means. I thought you were different." She then storms off murmuring.

Lena celebrates with Jonathan and says, "I knew you could do it."

Jonathan replies, "I couldn't do it without you."

Janelle walks up and says, "Let's solve for Y."

Lena says quickly in her, "I know you didn't" voice, "Excuse me?!" She says with a disgusted look on her face.

Janelle was a faithful church going woman. Prior to dating Jonathan, she was involved with drug dealers and men that had mental health disorders. She would always be inconsistent with him. At first she wanted to be friends then she'd want a relationship. After in the relationship, she would make claims that God told her that they shouldn't be together. Finally, she told Jonathan this and he was done with her. She called back after she realized that it wasn't God, it was her. He no longer fell for her tears and promises. She was mad at him. She felt like he should've forgiven her and got back into the relationship. Janelle says in a sinister and sadistic tone, "How soon we forget?" Lena points a finger at Jonathan and says, "You think you gone play me too! I got some math for you. I'm gonna subtract you from thoughts." She storms off.

Tasha is talking in a euphoric manner, "$1000. I can't believe it!"

Anthony jumps in and says, "What an upgrade I could get!"

Tasha giggles and says, "You love computers."

Janine was a girl from the projects. She was the type that was played by a lot of men in her past, so she decided to stop getting played and became the player. Anthony fell hard for her in the past. Janine walks up with a female super villain look in her eye and says, "How 'bout you upgrade me Pretty Tony!"

Tasha screams, "Pretty Tony? Pretty Tony? Pretty Tony?" She walks off waving them off.

The boys walk in with "I'm sorry" gifts. Girls are talking with ex-boyfriends. Donique says to Malik,

"Yeah I do like rough dudes."
Malik replies, "You my girl."

Lena says to Lance, "I like aggressive men."

Lance replies, "I know you do."

Tasha says to Tyrone, "I don't always want to talk."

Tyrone replies laughing a little, "Yeah you were trippin."

Keisha tells Chris, "I want to get gifts sometimes."

Chris replies, "Let me buy something."

The boys make eye contact with the girls as they walk into the room. They drop the "I'm sorry" gifts that they have in their hands, which include flowers, candy, cards, and teddy bears. Michael jumps in and says, "We're supposed to be the ones leading double lives and keeping secrets?!"

David replies, "Yeah let's go guys."

Donique yells to David, "Hold on Dave. Wait."

All the boys storm out one after the other. Keisha and the girls finish their discussions with their ex's.

Keisha speaks up, "Yeah, we do want me with a little hood in them."

Lena jumps in, "Yeah, but who still knows how to take care of their woman."

Tasha speaks up like a defense attorney, "Those other guys you just saw got hood in them."

Malik, Chris, Lance, and Tyrone all laugh. Malik jumps in sarcastically saying, "What they know 'bout hood." He laughs.

Chris cosigns on the fun, "Nothing, maybe Robin

Hood," he says as he laughs.

Tyrone is snickering, "Yeah."

Lance leading the charge says, "Let's go find someone new."

Malik, Tyrone, and Chris simultaneously say, "Yeah!!!"

Donique says, "Bye."

Lena has one hand on her hip, throws up the deuces, and says, "Holla!

The boys and girls are in their rooms trying to hold out the telephone rings. Donique asks, "we gon' answer it?"

Lena says, "No."

Tasha jumps in, "Yeah, don't answer it."

Keisha replies, "I don't know."

Keisha sneaks to restroom to call the boy's room. The telephone is ringing.

Anthony says, "Let's answer it."

David says, "No, let's be strong."

Michael jumps in with leader bass in his voice, "Yeah".

The phone rings constantly. The boys and girls try to be strong and go out, but they will be surprised.

Lena says in drained voice, "This party is lame."

Tasha agrees, "Yeah it is."

Keisha seconds the notion saying, "These brothas just ain't doin' it for me." Donique is so exhausted and surprisingly unable to talk. She utters, "Man".

The boys are standing around talking. You can see the "I don't belong here look" in their eyes. They are standing together uncomfortably in a group. Everyone around them are seated, laughing, and talking or circled up standing, engaging each other. The boys look like the poster children for exhaustion. Michael initiates, "Is it me or is this boring?"

Dave replies, "I don't think it's you."

Anthony replies, "Me neither."

Jonathan joins the pack, "I agree."

Anthony says with hope, "There they are." Seeing the group of girls.

David sees and agrees and says, "That is them."

Jonathan asks, "What do we do?"

Michael takes the initiative and hopes they will follow his example, "I don't know about y'all, but I'm about to man up!"

He walks up to the girls and the other guys follow. Keisha says, "Hi."

Michael replies excitedly, "Hi."

Keisha says, "Michael, I'm sorry about the other night. I'm just used to dating guys that let me down so are my girls."

Michael says, "Its ok. I should have told you about her. I won't let you down."

They give each other a long, tight hug.

David says, "Hey."

Donique asks, "What up?"

David says, "Donique, I know I think too much, and I'm confused about things a lot. One thing I'm not confused about is that I want you."

Donique says, "Aww, this feels like when they destroyed the Death Star." David is beyond amazed. This is an allusion and reference that shows that Donique was paying attention and comprehending the movie. She says to him, "If you ever try to leave me, I will break all your little Storm Trooper figurines! It'll look like a scene from a CSI version of Star Wars!"

David with his hand on his chest says, "Oh Donique! Come here my little hood girl." He gives her a quick kiss and a long, tight hug.

Jonathan says, "Hi, Lena."

Lena replies, "Hi, Jonathan."

Jonathan starts his apology speech, "Oh Lena. I think I'm so smart, but this one problem I couldn't solve."

Lena replies, "You are smart. Sometimes there are lurking variables."

Jonathan says, "I'm sorry Lena. Do you forgive me?"

"Yes my little math wiz," she replies then kisses him.

Anthony asks, "How you been?"

Tasha replies, "I been ok".

Anthony says, "I missed you."

Tasha admits, "I missed you too."

Anthony says, "I made glitch or mistake."

Tasha responds back, "I think we can reprogram this one". She smiles and hugs him.

The past love interests all walk in. Lance walks up and asks, "So it's like dat Lena? Y'all gon' leave us for these nerds."

Jonathan jumps in, "You had your chance. You blew it!"

Lance turns with chest out shouting, "Shut up punk!"

Asia interrupts the guys arguing, "So what's it gonna be Michael?"

Michael replies, "It's not gonna be."

David says, "I got your punk Negro! We 'bout to have to move some furniture back!"

Donique is shocked. She wasn't expecting that. He whistles and some other nerds walk up behind them with eyeglass cases.

Michael says, "Hold these." He and his boys hand their glasses to the other nerds and they start rolling up their sleeves.

Chris says, "It looks like Robin-hood and them think they bad."

Jonathan jumps in and says, "Spell Robin hood sucka!" He flinches at Chris.

Malik shouts, "I say we break these nerds off!"

360 walks up at that very moment and says, "Touch him and we'll break y'all off." He partially lifts his shirt. His other nickname should be 380 from what he's packing. The rest of 360's crew walks up. Malik quickly says, "We good. I ain't trying to get no blood on my new shoes no way!"

Lance talks to Asia in a sly manner, "Forget about him baby."

Asia says, "Yeah I will, but not you. What's your name?"

Lance introduces himself, "I'm Lance".

The ex-boyfriends and previous female potential loves walk off talking to each other.

Michael looks surprised and says, "What are y'all doing here?"

360 says, "We wanted someone new too."

A smart looking sophisticated girl with glasses and a pants suit looking like an attorney walks up. 360 introduces the mystery lady, "This is Christina."

Christina says, "Hi."

Michael says, "Hi."

Donique is watching the ex-boyfriends and ex-girlfriends walk off, "Well, looks like we're not the only ones trying something new."

David says, "Yeah well don't knock it till you've tried it."

Everyone laugh.

Michael decides to have a playful moment with the girls, "Well, ladies you know what it is. Once you go nerd you start enjoying things of which you never heard," he laughs.

All the other guys chime in, "Yeah." They start walking with glide in their stride. Keisha jumps in, "Now you know we ain't gonna sit back quietly after that one. Well, we brought THUG out of y'all."

Tasha jumped in, "Yeah that an acronym for "Tough Hard Uninhibited Geek".

Lena jumps in and says, "Yeah, we had y'all smiling like that disappearing cat from <u>Alice in Wonderland</u>."

They all crack up.

Donique says, "Now y'all know I was gonna put my 2 cents in. Now I did some data mining and me and my girls hacked y'all. The way y'all confronted our past boyfriends we said that was a little too street for just Crown-point. Try Parkside, Desoto Bass, and Summit Square. Don't hate the player hate the video game."

All her girls simultaneously start twiddling their thumbs like they were playing an Xbox. The boys just laugh. Tasha joins in the fun and says, "Now y'all walk over to y'all consoles and show us how much y'all love us."

Each guy walks up and starts passionately kissing his girl.

Epilogue

Bet you're wondering what happened. 360 ended up marrying Christina who turned out to be a member of front office for the Cleveland Cavaliers, so 360 ended up playing for the Cavs in the NBA. His boys ended up all playing in the NBDL, overseas, and for And 1. They are all happily married. Michael and Keisha, Lena and Jonathan, Tasha and Anthony, and Donique and David are all happily married as well. Nathan and Markita got married. Markita is now a counselor and job placement consultant for the "One More Gin", an agency that finds jobs for and places women that were previously incarcerated with jobs. Dr. Hampton ended up marrying her intern. They now run the Don't Knock it 'Till You Try it Get-Away and an online dating service that does psyche assessments to match couples. Ryan and Jade married and now run an accounting and financial firm that aids poor citizens to understand financial literacy.

The End

GREAT READS BY AMB PUBLISHING

NOW AVAILABLE THE JOURNEY THE TRUE STORIES OF 12 WOMEN, OF SURVIVAL, RECOVERY, AND REDEMPTION

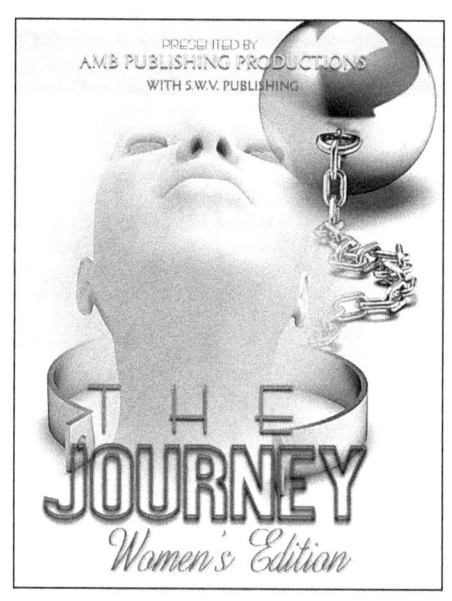